The Happy Hollisters on a River Trip

BY JERRY WEST

Illustrated by Helen S. Hamilton

GARDEN CITY, N.Y.

Doubleday & Company, Inc.

Printed in the United States of America

Contents

CHAPTER 1

A Clown Fish

RICKY HOLLISTER tiptoed across the lawn toward the side of his house. In his left hand he held a jar. In his right hand was the lid, full of holes.

Following Ricky was his sister Holly. "Will you catch him this time?" she asked excitedly.

"Sh! Don't make so much noise," her brother replied. "You can't catch a bee unless you're real quiet."

The seven-year-old boy kept his blue eyes on a big bumble bee which had lighted on a leaf of a bush. He moved slowly toward it, like a cat about to spring on a mouse.

Then quickly he clapped the buzzing bee into the jar and screwed on the lid.

"I have him! I have him!" Ricky shouted. He placed his freckled nose close to the jar. "See how he buzzes around in there!"

"What are you going to do with him?" Holly asked.

His sister, who was six, had dark hair, braided in pigtails. Her brown eyes sparkled, especially when she giggled at funny things her brother said.

Ricky had long legs, which were always in motion. His hair, which never stayed combed, was reddish in color. He had a turned up nose and a jolly grin. In answer to Holly's question he said:

"Oh, I'll watch the bee for awhile." He bent over to pull a handful of grass. "Let's make a bed for him."

Suddenly both children looked up as a strange car came into their driveway.

"Oh!" exclaimed Holly. "It's Patty Eldridge from Crestwood where we used to live."

Ricky set the jar down at the foot of the bush. Then he and Holly raced toward the car to greet Patty and her parents. The Hollisters had not seen them since they had moved from the town where they used to live.

The door of the car was flung open and blond-haired Patty, who was Holly's age, hopped out.

"Hello," the Hollisters said together.

"What are you going to do with him?"

"We surprised you," Patty said, dimpling. "We're driving back from our vacation. I asked Mommy and Daddy to stop and visit you, like you said in your letter, Holly."

"I'm so glad you did," Holly replied, hugging her.

"What a fine place you have here," Mr. Eldridge said, getting out of the car and glancing about at the big house with its wide lawns and trees. "You're right on the lake front, too. Do you have a boat?"

"Oh yes, and it's good fishing," Ricky cried. "Want to catch some?"

Mr. Eldridge laughed and tousled Ricky's hair. "Not yet, young man," he said with a chuckle. "Mrs. Eldridge and I would like to see your parents first."

Pretty, blond Mrs. Hollister, who had heard the talking, came out to the porch of the big white house to meet the Eldridges. At the same time, two other children on bicycles rode into the yard. One was ten-year-old Pam Hollister. Her fluffy golden hair was blowing in the breeze as she brought her bicycle to a sudden stop and smiled. Beside her was twelve-year-old Pete. He had blond hair with a crew cut and friendly blue eyes.

"Hello, Mr. and Mrs. Eldridge!" he called. "It's nice to see you again. How is everything in Crestwood?"

The man shook hands with the boy and said, "Well, the town is still there, but it's not the same since the Happy Hollisters left. And, Pete, I believe you've grown an inch since I last saw you."

The boys hopped on their bicycles to go fishing.

"Pam, too," Mrs. Eldridge said, as she kissed Pam.

Suddenly a little voice piped up behind them. "How about me? Have I grown any?"

It was Sue Hollister, the cute, dark-haired four-year-old baby of the family. Her daddy had told her only the night before that she was growing like a weed.

"Why, Sue," Mrs. Eldridge said, picking her up. "You'll soon be as tall as your mother."

Everybody laughed as they went into the house. After the girls had shown Patty their big colorful bedrooms, all of the children went outside to play.

Pete was about to step into their rowboat, which was tied to the family's dock at the rear of the long lawn at the back of the house when his mother called him. Pete hurried back to see what she wanted.

"I've asked the Eldridges to stay to supper," she

said. "We're having fish tonight, but I'm afraid there won't be enough. Since this is Wednesday, the stores are closed, Pete." Then Mrs. Hollister smiled. "Will you do me a favor?"

Her son knew immediately what his mother meant. "Catch more fish for you?" he asked.

His mother winked. "A couple of nice fat ones. Just the way you did last week."

Pete dashed off toward the garage to get his fishing tackle, at the same time calling his brother.

"Oh boy!" Ricky said, when he was asked to help. "Let's go! Shall we take the boat or our bikes?"

"Bikes. We'll go to that place on the Muskong River near the old dead tree. I think the fish are hanging around out there, and we'll have more luck."

The boys hopped onto their bicycles and fifteen minutes later reached the bank of the Muskong River which emptied out of beautiful Pine Lake. They baited their hooks and cast the lines into the swift running water. Ricky was the first to get a nibble.

"A perch!" cried Pete. "And a nice one, too!"

Suddenly there was a hard tug on Pete's pole. "I got something big!" he exclaimed, reeling it in.

The fish jumped and flopped about in the water, trying to get off the hook. Carefully Pete played it in and landed the fish on the shore.

"A Muskong bass!" he cried. "I'll bet it weighs four pounds."

The fish was an odd variety of bass found only in the Muskong River. It had white circles around its eyes, which had earned it the nickname of Clown Fish.

"Hey look, what's this?" Pete asked. Around the fish's tail was a metal band. On it was stamped, "Old Moe 122."

"A band on a fish's tail!" Ricky said. "What for?"

"Someone must have put the band on," replied Pete. "But I wonder what it means. Old Moe 122."

"Maybe it was stuck on by a man 122 years old," Ricky joked. "Here, let me see if we can get it off."

Pete already had taken the hook from the fish's mouth. As Ricky tried to remove the band, the bass gave a tremendous flip flop out of his hands and slid back into the river.

"Get him quick!" Ricky cried.

"Hey, look, what's this band?" Pete asked.

Pete thrust his arm into the water, but too late. The fish had zipped off into the deep river.

"Good night!" said Pete in disappointment.

"Well, we'll just have to catch another one," Ricky sighed.

This did not happen at once. But ten minutes later each boy caught a plump trout, and they decided to go home. As they turned to climb up the bank, they were surprised to see a boy sitting high on the river bank watching them.

He was a thin lad about ten years old, with sad brown eyes. His dungarees were tattered, and in one hand he held a basket half filled with vegetables and cookies.

"Hi, there," Pete called cheerfully. "You going fishing?"

Before the boy had time to reply, a roughly-dressed man appeared and began to scold him.

"Why aren't you selling the vegetables and cookies?" he shouted. "I agreed to keep you if you did some work. Get back to town!"

The boy mumbled a reply and scrambled to his feet. As the two disappeared down the trail, Ricky said, "What a nasty man!"

"Yes. Wouldn't it be awful to be treated like that?" Pete declared. Then he added, "We'd better hurry home."

When the boys arrived at their house, Mrs. Hollister smiled in pleasure.

"What a fine catch!" she said.

"Get back to town!"

It was not long before supper was ready. Mr. Hollister had arrived while Pete and Ricky were fishing. He was a tall rugged outdoor type of man, with brown wavy hair and laughing eyes. He had recently taken on the popular *Trading Post* in the town of Shoreham. This was a combination hardware, sporting goods and toy store.

During supper, the boys told about the big fish that had gotten away from Pete, and Mr. Hollister began to tease him as if he thought the bass were only a small one.

"But honest, Dad," Pete said, "it was a huge Clown Fish."

"But that band on its tail," Mr. Hollister said with a wink at Mr. Eldridge. "Are you sure about that?"

Both Pete and Ricky said indeed they were sure and what was more, they intended to find out who had put the band on the fish's tail.

"I hope you can," their father said.

Suddenly Pam had an idea. "Suppose we use the fish for another stunt to bring more business to *The Trading Post*," she said.

Only a short time before the Hollisters had dropped armfuls of balloons from a high church tower in the center of town. Some had contained notices of prizes. The children who found the balloons brought them to *The Trading Post* for their prizes.

"Another idea?" Mrs. Hollister said smiling at her daughter. "What is it, Pam?"

The girl put down her dessert spoon and said, "If Daddy puts a real large aquarium in the window of his store, maybe he can have a big fish contest."

"Hey, that's swell!" Pete cried.

"I'm going to catch the biggest fish," Ricky declared.

"No," Pam said. "This will be only for Daddy's customers. The one who catches the biggest fish in the Muskong River in two weeks wins a prize. How about it, Dad?"

"Wonderful," Mr. Hollister said. "There's a whopping glass aquarium in the basement of *The Trading Post*. We'll use that, and I'll offer a prize of twenty-five dollars worth of merchandise for the largest fish."

All the children became excited as plans were made

for the big fish contest. The Eldridges said they were sorry not to be able to stay until the contest would begin. It all sounded like wonderful fun, but they had to go home. They did stay overnight, however, and Patty slept with Holly.

Next morning after the Eldridges drove off, Pete and Ricky began talking about the Clown Fish that had got away. They were determined to find out more about the strange Old Moe whose name was on the tag, and went to ask some neighbors about it. When they questioned Mr. Smith, who was working in his garden near the lake front, the man smiled and said:

"Another Old Moe tag? Well, what do you know! I've heard about several of those. In fact, my brother caught a Clown Fish last year with a tag that said, 'Old Moe 36'."

"Gee, Old Moe got awful old in one year, didn't he?" Ricky said, and the others laughed.

"Hasn't anybody solved the mystery, Mr. Smith?" Pete asked.

"Not that I know of."

"I wish we could find Old Moe," Ricky said. "Maybe he could give us some of those nice fat Clown Fish."

"We'll catch some more ourselves," Pete said, "and put 'em in the aquarium to get people interested in the contest."

The boys spoke to their mother and then went back to the Muskong River. This time Pete caught a big Clown Fish, but it had no tag on its tail.

Carrying the pail carefully, he steered with one hand.

"He's a beauty, though," he said. "Let's take it to Dad."

The boys had brought a bucket with them. Pete put the fish into it and straddled his bike. Carrying the pail carefully in one hand, he steered with the other as they went toward *The Trading Post*.

When they arrived there, Mr. Hollister already had the aquarium set up in the window, full of water. Pete and Ricky parked their bikes alongside the building and were about to carry the fish inside when a boy approached them. He was Joey Brill, who had been making trouble for the Hollisters ever since they moved to Shoreham. He was Pete's age, but larger. With a sneer he said:

"What have you got in that pail?"

"A fish," Pete replied.

"Let me see it?"

"Okay, take a look." Pete set the pail down.

Joey looked into it and sneered. "You think that's a big fish? I can catch a better one in my gold fish bowl!"

"Go ahead," Ricky replied. "Nobody's stopping you."

He reached down to pick up the pail, but Joey laid a hand on his arm. "Here, let me carry it," he said. "I'm stronger than you are."

"You are not stronger than my brother," Ricky said hotly.

"Oh no? Then feel my muscle."

Joey flexed his arm, and as Ricky tried to feel his muscle, he gave him a hard push.

"Let my brother alone!" Pete warned.

But Joey had no intention of parting peaceably. He lunged at Pete. In doing so, he gave the pail a kick. It flew into the street directly in front of an oncoming car!

CHAPTER 2

A Store Contest

As THE Clown Fish flopped in the street in front of the car, the Hollister boys cried out. The driver saw the bass and the bucket, and swerved just in time.

Pete ran out to grab the fish but it kept slipping out of his hands. Ricky had picked up the bucket. Now he went to help his brother.

"Ho, ho, you'll never catch him!" called Joey and ran off.

Pete and Ricky paid no attention to him. They were too busy with the fish. Every time they touched it, the bass would give a tremendous leap.

"He'll wear himself out and die before we can get him into the aquarium," Pete groaned.

As he and Ricky were struggling to get hold of the fish, a boy who had been standing nearby put down a basket and a loaf of bread and hurried over to help. He was the same lad the mean man had scolded out on the bank of the river.

The boy moved quickly and seized the bass by the gills. With the three boys holding onto it, the fish finally stopped struggling and was carried into the store.

"Hi, Tinker!" Pete called to a tall man who was waiting on a customer. "Help us get this fish into the tank quick, will you?"

Tinker, a kind man whom Mr. Hollister had hired to help him at *The Trading Post*, excused himself from the customer and opened a little door at the back of the store window. The three boys stepped inside and put the fish into the aquarium.

"Is it dead?" Ricky asked, as the bass lay on its side and did not swim.

"I don't think so," Pete replied, prodding it a bit. "Look, his tail is moving."

As the three boys looked on, the fish began to move slowly. First it righted itself, then with a few more wiggles began to swim about normally.

"Whew!" said the boy who had helped them. "I never thought it would pull through."

"We wouldn't have made it if you hadn't run over to help us," said Pete gratefully. "Thanks a lot."

"What's your name?" Ricky asked him.

"Bobby Reed." The boy smiled. "I've heard about you fellows. You're the Hollister boys, aren't you? The Happy Hollisters?"

"Yes. I'm Pete, and this is Ricky."

"I think Joey Brill spilled the pail on purpose," Bobby said.

"I know," Pete replied. "We've had trouble with him before."

When the Hollisters first came to Shoreham, Joey

had tried to scare them by saying their house was haunted.

"Well, when Joey sees the fish alive in the aquarium, he'll know his trick didn't work," Ricky said.

The boys stepped down through the little door from the show window into the store. They almost bumped into Pam Hollister who was carrying a big piece of cardboard, a pencil and a paint brush.

"What's that for?" Ricky asked.

"You watch."

Pam leaned on a counter and began to sketch letters onto the cardboard with a pencil. She looked up.

"Oh, it's going to be a sign announcing the big fish contest," Pete said, and told Bobby about it.

They watched Pam as she sketched out the big

They watched as Pam sketched big letters.

block letters. Then she painted the sign, being careful to keep the letters even.

"That's swell!" Pete exclaimed, admiring the finished sign. It read:

BIG FISH CONTEST

$25.00 worth of merchandise
for the person catching the
largest bass in Muskong River.

Contest will continue for two weeks.

BRING THEM BACK ALIVE!

In a few minutes, the sign had dried, and Pete put it in the store window next to the aquarium. Immediately a crowd began to gather outside. The Hollister children went out to listen to their comments.

"Well, well," said a fat man, "I can catch a fish bigger than that one."

"Me, too," boasted another.

A tall boy said, "What am I waiting for? I'm going to get my fishing pole and catch one right away." As the others laughed, he hurried off.

When Pete looked around, he suddenly realized that Bobby was not in sight.

"Where did Bobby go?" he asked Ricky.

"I don't know, but look. There's his loaf of bread

that he laid on the sidewalk. I guess he only took his basket."

Pete picked up the bread which was in a waxed paper marked Miller's Bakery.

"He must have been on an errand when he stopped to help us," Pete said.

When he told Pam about it, she suggested that he take the bread to his house.

"But I don't know where he lives," Pete said.

Pam glanced down the street. "Here comes Dave Mead," she said. "Perhaps he knows."

Dave was a tall, good-looking boy of Pete's age whom the children had met at a party soon after they moved into town. His straight, black hair always hung down over his forehead no matter how often he combed it.

When Pete asked him if he knew Bobby Reed, he said, yes, he did. Bobby and his mother, who were poor, lived in a shack down by the Muskong River. It was not far from the Stone Bridge.

"You can't miss it," Dave said, "because it has a red brick chimney that's falling apart."

Pete and Pam decided to walk there and return the bread. Ricky said he wanted to go home to play ball with some of his friends. Dave agreed to accompany him on Pete's bike and take the pail back.

"See you later," Pete said, as he and Pam set off to find Bobby Reed's house.

It was not long before the two children came to the

path which led toward the river. Soon they were in sight of the Stone Bridge.

"Oh, look," Pam said, pointing toward the river. "I think that's our dog." Among the bushes at the water's edge, the children saw a dog's tail wagging back and forth.

"It's Zip all right," Pete said. "He's chasing frogs again."

Zip was the Hollisters' faithful collie. He often accompanied the children on their adventures, and on more than one occasion had saved them from trouble.

Pete thrust two fingers into his mouth and gave a sharp whistle. The tail stopped wagging, and the dog looked around. When he saw the children, he bounded up to meet them.

"He'd like to chase a stick in the river."

"Hi!" Pete said, stroking Zip's head. "How's the frog hunting today?"

The dog licked Pete's hands and started back toward the river, barking.

"I know what he wants," Pam said. "He'd like to chase a stick in the river."

She and Pete ran along behind the dog until they came to the river bank. Pete picked up a short stick and threw it far out into the stream. Zip dashed into the water after it. Swimming with strong strokes, the dog reached the stick, snapped it into his mouth, and started back to shore.

When he was nearly there, he stopped to look at something half-submerged in the water. The children saw that it was an old rowboat. On the prow of the boat, next to an iron anchor ring, sat a turtle, sunning itself.

With a turn of his head and a quick look at the children, Zip let go of the stick and swam toward the old boat.

"He's going to try to catch the turtle," Pam said, laughing.

But Zip was too noisy. The turtle slipped over the side of the boat and disappeared into the water. Zip splashed around for a minute, then retrieved the stick and brought it to the feet of the children.

"Good boy," Pam said. "Goodness! Don't shake that water off on me."

After Pam threw the stick into the river again and

"This boat hasn't been used in a long time."

Zip dashed off to get it, Pete looked at the old row-boat.

"I wonder who owns it," he said.

"It looks as if it's been abandoned," his sister replied.

"If it doesn't belong to anybody," Pete went on, "Ricky and I might fix it up. I think I'll look it over."

He laid the bread on the bank, then removed his shoes and socks and rolled up his dungarees. Wading into the water, he grabbed the anchor ring to which a rusty chain was attached. As he pulled up the anchor, which was covered with weeds, Pete said:

"This boat hasn't been used in a long time. No wonder it's so waterlogged."

He pulled the boat up to the shore to get a better look at it. All the floor boards seemed to be in place.

"Let's turn it over to get the water out," Pam suggested. "I'll help you."

Zip barked a couple of times as if to say he wanted them to play with him instead. But he wagged his tail and watched as Pete and Pam tilted the boat on its side. The water poured out with a rush.

"Okay. Let it fall back. One, two, three!"

The bottom of the boat slapped the water, and it was afloat.

"Hey, not bad!" Pete exclaimed. "It leaks but the holes could be plugged up. I'm going to paddle around in it."

Seeing a long thin piece of wood on the shore, he picked it up for a paddle.

"Jump in, Pam. I'll take you for a ride," he offered. When Zip whimpered, he added, "You too, pal. Hop aboard."

Zip bounded into the front of the boat, and Pam sat on the center seat. Pete pushed the boat out a little way, scrambled into the stern and started to paddle.

"This is leaking pretty badly," Pam said, taking off her shoes. "We'd better not go far."

"You're right. It'll take a lot of bailing to keep this old tub afloat."

Pete paddled in a big circle and headed back to shore.

" Hurry!" Pam said, as the water began to come in faster.

Pete paddled with all his might and soon the bow

scraped on the shore. By this time it was half-filled with water.

"Crickets," Pete exclaimed as they got out. "This crate needs a lot of fixing."

He pushed the boat out a way and threw the anchor into the water. The children put on their shoes and started off again. They had just passed under the Stone Bridge, when Pam said:

"I see a red chimney, Pete. Over there!"

Up ahead they could glimpse an old shack nestled among trees on high ground. Reaching it, they noticed neat flowered curtains at the windows, but otherwise the house looked dilapidated. Its roof sagged, and the yellow paint was flaking off.

The children were about to walk up to the door when they heard shouts from the rear.

"Hurry," Pam said, as the water came in faster.

"I don't have any!" somebody shouted angrily.

Another voice said loudly, "Yes you do! Give me some of them, or I'll hit you!"

This was followed by a rustling in the bushes, and Bobby Reed rushed out. His face was red, and he was out of breath. In one hand, he clutched his basket.

"Bobby!" Pete called out. "We're looking for you. Did—"

But the panting boy was too terrified to pay any attention.

Racing toward the house, he glanced back over his shoulder. In doing this the boy did not see a stick lying in his path. He stepped on it and slipped to one knee. The basket nearly flew out of his hand.

"Oh!" cried Pam, fearing that Bobby had hurt himself.

The boy scrambled to his feet again and scooted toward the house. But as he raced forward, a stone shot out from the bushes.

It flew directly toward Pam's head!

CHAPTER 3

Stung!

PETE saw the stone out of the corner of his eye.

"Duck, Pam!" he shouted.

His sister moved just in time, and the stone sailed over her head. The thrower came in sight. Joey Brill!

Bobby Reed raced up to them. He was being chased by Joey, who was throwing more stones.

"Help!" Bobby shouted. "Help!"

When Joey saw the Hollister children, he was so surprised that he stopped short. This gave Pete a chance to act quickly. Before Joey could throw another stone, Pete flung himself at the boy. Together they rolled over and over on the ground.

Although Joey was a larger boy, Pete was quicker. He got to his feet immediately, and when Joey rose, Pete punched him on the nose.

"Ow!" Joey cried. "That's no fair. Three against one. I'll get even with you!" He ran off down the path toward the Stone Bridge.

Now that the troublesome bully was gone, Pete and Pam turned their attention to Bobby. He had fled to the shack and was standing by the front door.

"What happened?" Pete asked, walking over to him.

Bobby said Joey often bothered him, especially since he had been selling vegetables and cookies for Farmer Gillis.

"He eats the cookies," Bobby said, "and Mr. Gillis punishes *me*. When Joey saw me this time, I'd sold all the cookies. It made him mad."

"He would do that to a smaller kid!" Pete exclaimed in disgust.

"Well, for once he didn't get away with it," Bobby said. "Thanks for helping me."

"Glad to," Pam said, adding, "You helped us. Is this your loaf of bread?"

"Yes, it is. Thanks," Bobby replied. "I left it in front of your store, didn't I?"

"Is it for your mother?" Pam asked.

"No. It's for Mr. Gillis. Mother's not here," the boy said sadly. "She has gone away, and I came here to see if there was any mail. I'm staying with Farmer Gillis until she returns. But he treats me awful mean."

Bobby said that he and his parents had lived on a farm out West. His dad had died, and Mrs. Reed was not strong enough to run the farm alone.

"Mother decided to write to my great grandfather who lived in Shoreham. He's our only relative. His name is Moses Twigg."

When Pete and Pam heard this, they looked at each other in surprise. Could Moses Twigg possibly be the Old Moe who put tags on fish?

Bobby continued his story, saying that his mother had written to Moses Twigg asking if she and Bobby might come East and help him with the fish and game store that he had owned for many years.

"But my great grandfather never answered her letter," the boy said. "So Mother thought we'd better come to Shoreham and talk things over with him. It took most of our money to buy the train tickets."

"Did you find him?" Pam asked eagerly.

"No," Bobby replied. "Great Grandpa Twigg's fish and game store burned down some years ago, we were told. He disappeared mysteriously, and nobody has heard from him since."

"Oh, how awful!" Pam exclaimed.

"Why did your mother leave here?" Pete asked.

"I hope Mother comes real soon," he cried.

Bobby said she had gone out West again to look for work, and had left him with Farmer Gillis. When she got a job and saved some money, she was to return and take Bobby away.

"I hope she comes real soon," he said, tears spilling from his eyes. "Mr. Gillis isn't nice to me. The only one on the farm who likes me is Mrs. Bindle, the housekeeper."

"Let's go and see her," Pam suggested. "Maybe she'll let you come over to our house to play and have lunch."

Bobby brightened at the idea, and the children hurried to the Gillis farm, which was a mile away. Mrs. Bindle was a stout, motherly woman, who said Bobby might visit the Hollisters. He looked happier than he had at any time since they had met him.

When the children arrived home, they were amused to see little Sue Hollister, and a roly-poly two-year-old boy named Stevie, who lived several houses away, trying to play croquet.

Stevie was bending far over using his own pudgy little hands rather than the mallet to push the ball through the wicket. Sue was struggling hard to show him how to strike the ball with a mallet.

"No, no, Tee-vee do it this way," the tiny fellow said firmly, throwing a ball through a wicket.

"I guess he's just too little," Sue sighed as she saw the others.

At this moment, Stevie's mother came to the rear door of her home.

He sat there, refusing to budge.

"Stevie!" she called. "Stevie!"

When the little fellow paid no attention, Sue said, "Your mother wants you."

She took him by the hand and gently tried to pull him in the direction of his own yard. But the chubby boy did not want to go home and sat down so hard on the green grass that Sue lost her balance and fell on top of him. She got up and tried hard to pull him up, but he sat there, refusing to budge.

"No go home," he insisted.

"Stee-vee!" his mother's voice rang out in alarm.

All this time Pete, Pam and Bobby watched the little scene, trying not to laugh. It was so funny that finally they all began to giggle.

Pam stepped forward and said, "Sue, we'll be glad to help you, dear."

"No," Sue replied firmly. "He's my playmate, and I'll take him home all by myself."

She thought hard for a couple of moments, and finally exclaimed, "Oh, I have a good idea! Maybe I can get him home with a sugar cookie!"

Sue raced into the kitchen and returned with a large one. As soon as Stevie saw it, he rose from the grass and walked toward her as fast as his pudgy little legs could go.

"Stevie want a cookie?" Sue coaxed.

She held it out just beyond his reach and began to walk rapidly in the direction of his house. Stevie hungrily followed after the outstretched hand with the cookie in it.

"Here, Stevie! Here, Stevie!" Sue called out to him.

She kept going in this fashion until the boy had safely reached his own yard. His mother laughed and thanked Sue, who now handed Stevie the cookie. Then the little girl ran back as fast as she could to her own yard where the other children were waiting for her to join them at lunch.

Pete had introduced Bobby to Mrs. Hollister, and told her about his missing great grandfather.

The children sat down to a delicious lunch of soup and roast beef sandwiches.

"What's for dessert?" Ricky asked eagerly.

His mother said that was a surprise, and in a few minutes she served them large bowls of ice cream. Bobby laughed and said he had not had so much fun in a long time. When they finished, the children helped clear the table, then went outside to play.

Suddenly Holly cried out in dismay. "Oh, that Joey!" she said. "I knew he was up to something."

The boy was hammering a croquet wicket into the ground!

"Stop that!" Pete cried, going toward him.

Joey dashed around the side of the house, with Zip barking at his heels. Suddenly he tripped over the jar which Ricky had set near a bush. *The jar in which he had trapped a bee!*

The lid flew off, and the bee buzzed out. As Joey ran, it lighted on his ankle and stung him.

"Oh! Ow!" he cried.

Thinking there might be more bees, Joey dashed

Joey ran around the house with Zip at his heels.

out of the yard as fast as he could and headed for his own home.

As the children watched him go, Mrs. Hollister opened the door and said there was a telephone call for Pete. He went inside.

The call was from Tinker. He said that two people had brought in fish bigger than Pete's, and that the whole town was talking about the contest.

"I thought maybe you'd like to come down and look at them," he said.

"I sure would," Pete replied.

When he told the others, all the children said they wanted to see the fish. Bobby was particularly enthusiastic. He seemed to have forgotten all his troubles and dashed from the front door with the Hollisters.

Then suddenly a look of fright came over his face. He stopped running and stared toward a car which had just parked in front of the house.

"What's the matter?" Pam asked him, noticing the strange look in his eyes.

"I—I'm afraid I'm in for trouble," Bobby said. He pointed. "That's Mr. Gillis getting out of the car."

The other children had stopped short too. They stood quietly as the man started up the walk. He paid no attention to the Hollisters; in fact, he walked right past them. Grasping Bobby by the shoulder, he said in an angry voice:

"What do you mean by coming here, you little scamp! You're supposed to be downtown selling vegetables and cookies for me!"

"Don't you ever try to see Bobby again!"

Bobby tried to explain that Mrs. Bindle had said he could come and have lunch with his new friends, but Mr. Gillis hardly paid any attention to him.

"Mrs. Bindle isn't in charge," he shouted. "I am. Your mother expects you to be of some use while you're staying at my house. Now come along with me."

He started pushing Bobby toward the car, but suddenly he stopped and faced the Hollister children.

"You're to blame for this!" he roared. "You stay out of my business. And don't you ever try to see Bobby again or you'll be sorry!" he thundered at them.

He shoved Bobby into the car and slammed the door. Then he went around to the driver's seat, got in, and roared off down the street.

The Hollister children looked at one another. Finally Holly said:

"Mr. Gillis is a mean man!"

"I'll say he is, treating Bobby like that," Pam agreed.

"I'm going to tell Mother," Holly said. She hurried into the house and reappeared with Mrs. Hollister.

"Can't you make that man be nice to Bobby Reed, Mother?" she was saying.

"I wish I'd seen him," Mrs. Hollister sighed. "Perhaps I could have persuaded Mr. Gillis to let Bobby stay."

"We could have bought all his cookies," Pam said. "Why didn't we think of that sooner?"

"I'm afraid it's too late now," her mother said.

All the children were dejected, thinking what might happen to their friend.

"Oh, I do hope he doesn't get a spanking," Pam said fervently.

"Poor Bobby!" Holly burst out. "Do you think Mr. Gillis meant what he said that we never can see Bobby again?"

CHAPTER 4

Escaped Animals

ALL the Hollister children felt so sorry for Bobby Reed that they did not even want to go downtown and look at the new fish in their father's aquarium. But their mother insisted they should go, because Tinker had asked them to.

"I wish we could do something for Bobby," Pam said. "But what could it be?"

None of them could think of anything right now, but they would not give up trying. Next morning Pete and Ricky decided to go fishing while they figured out a plan.

After the boys had set off, Pam and Holly helped their mother tidy the kitchen. While working, they began to talk about the mysterious Old Moe, who put tags on fish.

"That's another little mystery for you to figure out," Mrs. Hollister said, thinking of the one the children had solved in connection with their house.

"I'm really going to find out who he is, Mother," Pam said.

Holly's eyes grew serious as she exclaimed, "Maybe

"Old Moe may live in town," Pam said.

Old Moe is in trouble and is trying to send a message on the tails of fish."

"Let's hunt for him," Pam said eagerly.

"But where?"

"For all we know, Old Moe may live right here in town," Pam said. "Sometimes missing people are found very near where they used to live, aren't they, Mother?"

"Yes, usually though, they're found in faraway places, so don't be discouraged if you don't succeed in locating him right away. But good luck to you."

The two girls left the house, hand in hand. First they stopped at the Hunters' to find out what they knew. Jeff and Ann said that they had never heard of anybody named Old Moe, but they would ask their mother. Mrs. Hunter said no, that she knew of no one by that name.

"But there is a man in town who knows just about everybody," Mrs. Hunter said. "He might be able to tell you."

"Who is he?" Pam asked.

"Mr. Lewis, the bus driver. Whenever anybody wants to find out where a person lives, he always asks Mr. Lewis."

"That's a good idea," Holly said. "Let's wait until he drives by next time. We'll stop him and ask if he knows Old Moe."

Jeff said that Mr. Lewis had driven by about fifteen minutes ago and was not due back for another half hour.

In the meantime the children played badminton in the Hunters' back yard. Pam and Holly were very good at it, and teamed up to beat Ann and Jeff. Finally Jeff looked at his wrist watch.

"Mr. Lewis should be here any time now," he said. "Let's go out front and watch for him."

As Jeff reached a spot where he could look down the road, he called, "Here he comes." The bus appeared far down the street.

The children ran to the corner stop and waited. When the bus stopped, Mr. Lewis opened the door.

"All you children want a ride?" He smiled.

"No," Ann replied. "We'd like to ask you some questions, Mr. Lewis."

"Go ahead," the driver said. "But make it snappy.

"We'd like to ask some questions, Mr. Lewis."

I don't have much time. I tell you, suppose you hop on the bus, and I'll give you a free ride for a couple of blocks while you ask your questions."

Holly giggled. What fun! The children got on the bus and sat down near the door.

"Now, what are your questions?" Mr. Lewis said as he started up.

Pam asked, "Do you know anybody in this town named Moe?"

"Moe?" Mr. Lewis scratched his head. "I know a Joe, and a Flo, but I don't know a—" He snapped his fingers. "Yes I do! I know a man named Moe."

Pam and Holly sat on the edge of their seats to hear more.

"You do?" Pam burst out. "Who is he and where does he live?"

"Is he old?" Holly asked.

"These questions are coming faster than traffic signals," Mr. Lewis said with a chuckle. "The Moe I know runs a barber shop. If you'll stay on my bus, I'll take you to his door."

"But we haven't any money with us," Pam said.

"The whole ride is on me," Mr. Lewis replied with a twinkle, and dropped four coins in the box.

Several other persons got on and off the bus before Mr. Lewis stopped near the center of town.

"There's Old Moe's place right across the street," he said. "I hope he's the man you're looking for."

The children thanked the bus driver and got off. They went across the street and on the window of the barber shop saw a sign "Moe's Place." When the children went inside they were met by a short, smiling man. He had a heavy black mustache but only a few hairs on the top of his head.

"Are you Old Moe?" Pam asked.

"Yes I am," he replied in a squeaky voice. "I suppose your sister wants a hair cut." He looked directly at Holly, who wore her hair in two long pigtails.

"Oh, no!" she exclaimed, grabbing her shiny braids. "You mustn't cut these off!"

The man frowned. "Then who does want a hair cut?" he asked.

"Nobody," Pam replied. "All we want to know is, Mr. Moe, do you keep fish?"

The barber's eyes brightened. "So you have heard about my fish, eh? Would you like to see them? Follow me."

42

As the children followed the man to the back of the shop, Holly whispered excitedly to Pam, "At last we've found Old Moe! Isn't it wonderful!"

The barber pointed to a small aquarium in a corner of the room.

"There are my fish," he said. "Aren't they little beauties?"

The young callers looked into the tank, which was full of tiny fish no bigger than a fly.

"These are guppies," he said.

The children said they were very nice, but they meant big fish like those in their father's store.

"They're a million times bigger than the guppies," Holly said.

"I guess you're not the Old Moe we're looking

"All we want to know is, do you keep fish?"

for," Pam said. "The man we want puts tags on fishes' tails, big fish that you catch in the Muskong River."

The barber said that he did not do this, and had never heard of anyone who did. Pam told him about their search to find out who was tagging the fish, and why.

The barber suggested that if they wanted to find out about Old Moe they should see the Wild Life Editor of the *Shoreham Eagle*. The newspaper office was located a short distance down the street. The children thanked him and left.

Jeff and Ann said they must go home. "I hope you find the right Old Moe," said Jeff. "Let us know."

"We will."

They had not gone far before they met Pete and Ricky. The boys had caught two beautiful rainbow trout, which they had taken to *The Trading Post* to put in the aquarium.

"They're not big enough to win a prize," Ricky said, "but it was fun."

When he and Pete heard the story from their sisters about the wrong Old Moe they had called on, the boys laughed. As it was noontime, the children returned home for lunch. Later they all walked to the newspaper office.

Entering the *Shoreham Eagle*, Pam stepped up to a young woman seated at a desk near the door.

"Is there something I can do for you?" she asked.

"Yes," Pam replied, and told her they would like to speak to the Wild Life Editor.

44

"Mr. Kent is the man you're looking for," said the young lady. "Would you like to go up?"

"Oh yes, we would," replied Pam.

The receptionist smiled and showed them where the stairway was. As the children climbed the steps, they suddenly heard a loud, roaring noise. At first, Holly wanted to dash out of the office, but a man who hurried past assured her that everything was all right. He said it was only the noise of the newspaper press starting up.

When the Hollisters got to the second floor they saw an office with Mr. Kent's name on the door. Pete opened it, and they went inside.

The man was not there, but a note on his desk read, "I will be right back."

The children sat down to wait for him. The newspaper building smelled strange, Pam said, and Pete told her it was probably the ink that was used to print the paper.

"This is a funny kind of office," Holly said, glancing around.

The walls were covered with mounted fish, deer heads and pictures of hunting trips. On one corner of Mr. Kent's desk was a stuffed owl.

"It looks more like a zoo," Ricky said, "but I like zoos." All at once he exclaimed, "Yikes! What's that?" and pointed to a cage on a low table behind Mr. Kent's desk.

The children walked over to it.

"A menagerie!" Pete exclaimed. "And these ani-

45

mals aren't stuffed. They're alive," he added as two sleepy opossums opened their eyes.

On top of a bookcase was an aquarium. It was made of glass and had a screen over the top. Inside there were a few clumps of ferns that grew between pretty-colored rocks. On one of the rocks sat the biggest frog the children had ever seen.

"Wow! That must be a great-grandfather like Old Moses Twigg," Holly said.

Beside the big frog were two lizards and a garter snake, which slithered around the sides of the aquarium.

"This is keen," Ricky said. "I want to get a better look at that frog."

He pushed his face close to the glass. "The frog is grinning at me," he said.

"The frog is grinning at me," Ricky said.

"I don't think we should get too nosy," Pete warned. "After all, this is Mr. Kent's office and we don't even know him."

Pam agreed with her brother. They should sit quietly until the editor returned.

They did this for a while, but soon Ricky became restless. He got up to look out the window. Then he went back to the aquarium.

"I'd like to pet that frog," he said.

Before Pam could tell him to leave it alone, her brother lifted the screened lid and put his hand in to touch the frog.

"Don't!" Pam exclaimed.

But it was too late. The frog gave a spring, leaping over Ricky's head and landed on the editor's desk.

As Ricky and the others turned to see where the frog had landed, the lizards crawled up the stiffest stems of the clump of ferns and slithered out. The next instant the snake wiggled to the top of the bookcase and started for the floor!

CHAPTER 5

A Mysterious Message

WHAT confusion there was! The big frog hopped wildly about. The lizards scampered under Mr. Kent's desk, and the garter snake disappeared in a pile of papers alongside the typewriter.

"Now you've done it!" Holly said.

"I didn't mean to," Ricky replied tearfully, as he tried to catch the frog.

Just then two men came into the office. Seeing the Hollisters dodging from place to place, they stared in amazement.

"Hey! What's going on here?" said one of them, a tall sun-tanned man.

"They all got loose," Holly explained. "My brother did it, but he's sorry."

"I see," the man said. Then he laughed. "I guess they're glad to be out."

The other man, who was slender and wore glasses, chuckled. "There's always something going on in your office, Mr. Kent."

The two men scampered about with the children, trying to catch the runaway creatures. At first they had no luck, but finally Holly picked up an empty wastebasket and captured the frog.

"Your hopping is over," she cried jubilantly, reaching under the wastebasket and catching the frog by one leg.

This was easy for her because she had learned from her brothers how to catch frogs on the lake shore. Mr. Kent lifted the lid of the aquarium, and Holly dropped the animal in.

The lizards were so nearly the color of the rug that it was hard to find them. The children and the two men crawled around looking under every piece of furniture.

Finally Ricky found one of the lizards in a corner near the file cabinet, and managed to grab it just before it squeezed behind the cabinet.

"Here's the other!" Pam cried.

She was over by the window and had suddenly seen the lizard climbing up a fold of the curtain. He was nearly out of reach, but she succeeded in catching him.

"Whew!" said Ricky. "This is just like a Wild West round-up."

The snake was harder to find. But Pete spied it about to slither in beside the opossums and picked it up.

When all the reptiles were restored to their home, and the screen top put on tightly, Mr. Kent laughed and said:

"My wife warned me not to keep these critters in the office. I guess it serves me right."

Finally Holly captured the frog.

Ricky apologized for letting the Wild Life Editor's pets escape.

"Don't worry about it," Mr. Kent replied, putting his hand on Ricky's head. "You can make up for it by finding me a lopadupolus."

"What's that?" Ricky said, not realizing he was being teased.

"You'll know when you find one," Mr. Kent said with a grin. "It's a first cousin to a thingamajig."

Ricky caught on and laughed too. Mr. Kent sat down in his desk chair and asked the others to seat themselves. There were not enough chairs for everybody, so the boys sat on the arms of the girls' chairs.

"Now what can I do for you children?" the editor asked.

Pete introduced himself, his brother and sisters,

and told the man they were there to ask him a question.

"This is my friend Mr. Finder," Mr. Kent said. "He works at the bank, but likes to come over to talk to me about fishing."

"That's what we want to talk to you about," Pete said. He told about catching the tagged Clown Fish. "We want to find out who Old Moe is for a very special reason," he added. "Do you happen to know him?"

The editor said he was sorry he did not. He would like very much to find out himself; it would make a very good newspaper story.

"From time to time we've had tagged fish reported to us," he said, "but no one has been able to solve the mystery of who Old Moe is."

"We think we might have a clue," Pam spoke up. "Did you ever hear of Moses Twigg who disappeared?"

The two men exchanged glances, and Mr. Finder asked Pam why she thought this was a clue. She told the story about Bobby Reed and his mother and how they had not heard from his great grandfather in a long time. Since he was a great fisherman, he might have gone off all by himself to do some experiments with fish.

"What kind of experiments?" Mr. Kent asked, now intensely interested.

Pam said she did not know exactly—maybe he

51

"You little folks have the best idea yet!"

wanted to see how big the fish would grow or something like that if they were not caught.

"But a few got away," Pete added.

Mr. Kent thumped the desk with his fist. He smiled at the Hollister children and said, "Well, of all things! The fishermen around this area have been trying for years to solve the mystery, and you little folks come up with the best idea yet."

"Only we can't find Old Moe," said Holly. "Couldn't you help us?"

While Mr. Kent was thinking this over, his friend from the bank spoke up. "This is all very strange," he said. "I came over here to put an advertisement in the newspaper about Moses Twigg."

The children looked at him in surprise, asking why he was doing this.

"When Moses Twigg disappeared," he said, "he left a sizeable account in our bank. We'd like to know very much if he's still alive. If not, the money should go to his heirs."

"Oh, it would go to Bobby and his mother!" Pam cried, "and they need it so much!"

Mr. Finder took a notebook from his pocket and jotted down the address of the little shack where the boy and his mother lived. He said that as soon as Mrs. Reed returned, he would get in touch with her. If the Hollisters could find out from Bobby when this would be, would they please let him know?

They promised to do so. Then Mr. Finder pulled another piece of paper from his pocket which he said was the ad, and laid it on Mr. Kent's desk. The editor read it aloud:

"Reward to anyone furnishing information about Moses Twigg, a former resident of Shoreham."

"A reward!" Pete almost shouted. "I'd like to win that reward!"

Mr. Finder smiled. "At the rate you're going, it wouldn't surprise me if you did win it," he said. "Well, I must be going now. Take care of the ad for me, will you, Mr. Kent?"

He stood up and the children also arose. They realized that they had already taken enough of the editor's time. He walked to the door with them, then suddenly asked if they had ever visited a newspaper office before. When they said no, he offered to show them around.

"How would you like to follow Mr. Finder's ad from start to finish?" he suggested.

"Oh, that would be wonderful!" Pam replied.

Mr. Kent picked up his telephone and the children heard him order someone to stop the presses. At once the great noise and roar, which they had heard and which was shaking the building a little, stopped.

"Follow me!" he said, and led the way downstairs.

First he took them to a desk where a young man sat and introduced him as the Advertising Manager. The man wrote okay on the advertisement Mr. Finder had left and handed it back to Mr. Kent.

Next they walked over to a type-setting machine. The fingers of the man working at it moved so fast that the children's eyes could hardly follow them. He stopped working and turned around.

"Will you set this up right away, please?" the editor asked him.

The man took the copy and in less than a minute had it ready. The advertisement dropped into a little slot, and Mr. Kent asked Ricky if he would like to carry it to the next place. He explained that it was too hot to be held and offered the boy his handkerchief to wrap it in.

They all walked over to the huge printing press which was now quiet. Mr. Kent told the man in charge that he was going to substitute the advertisement for something else on the front page. The man looked quickly over the big metal plate and pulled out three lines of type from the bottom of it. Quickly he inserted the copy about Moses Twigg. Then Mr. Kent told him to go ahead.

The man clicked a switch and at once the big press started rolling again. The noise was so great that Holly put her hands over her ears. This made the editor and the other man laugh.

"If you were around here long, you'd get used to this," Mr. Kent said. Then turning to Pete, he asked, "How would you like to have the first paper off the press with the ad in it about Moses Twigg? You can take it home."

Pete was thrilled by the idea and followed Mr. Kent to the far end of the big press where the finished newspapers had once more started coming out of the machine neatly folded and ready to be shipped out.

They reached the spot just as the paper with the

They reached the press as the ad came through.

new ad in it came from the press. Pete picked it up, and read the ad aloud.

"Well, here's hoping you win the reward!" Mr. Kent smiled.

Then he said good-by, and the children left the newspaper office. The Hollisters hurried home and excitedly showed the paper to their mother, declaring that they were not going to give up until they had found Moses Twigg. They also hoped he would be Old Moe, so they could solve two mysteries at once.

"That surely would be thrilling," Mrs. Hollister said. "By the way, Pete, there was a telephone call for you a little while ago. The speaker didn't say who he was. Just said he'd call later."

At that moment the phone rang. Pete answered it and heard a strange, high-pitched voice that sounded a little like a woman say:

"I hear you want to know something about Old Moe."

Pete was excited. "Yes, I do. You know something about him?"

"Uh huh. I'll tell you a secret if you'll meet me at the Stone Bridge in a few minutes."

Before Pete could ask the person's name, the stranger had hung up. Pete reported the message to his mother and asked permission to go to the Stone Bridge. Mrs. Hollister frowned, saying this was a rather irregular procedure.

"But we ought to investigate it, don't you think?" Pete asked.

They clung to the bank under the bridge.

"That's right," Pam added. "If we're going to be good detectives, Mother, we shouldn't overlook a single clue. I'll go with Pete."

Mrs. Hollister agreed, but cautioned, "Good detectives also must be careful."

Pam and Pete promised not to get into any danger, and were about to set off when Ricky begged to go along. Then Holly said she wanted to be with them if there was going to be an adventure.

"And me, too," Sue insisted.

Mrs. Hollister smiled. "The more, the safer it is, I suppose," she said, and gave her consent. The five children trooped off excitedly, with Pam taking little Sue by the hand. They crossed a field and followed a path that led to the Stone Bridge.

In a little while they reached the river bank and

soon they came to the old Stone Bridge. The children looked around, but could see no one.

"Maybe that strange person decided not to meet us after all," said Pam.

"Maybe we got here ahead of him," Pete suggested.

They waited for several minutes. When no one came, Holly suggested that maybe the person meant the other side of the bridge.

"We'll walk over there," said Pete. "Don't step in the water."

They clung to the bank as they went under the bridge. Just as they reached the other side, a deep voice boomed out from somewhere above them.

"I'm Old Moe!"

This was followed by a high-pitched laugh, which frightened them. Sue grabbed Pam. Holly and Ricky began to shake.

"I'm Old Moe!" the voice said again.

The children looked up to the top of the bridge. With that something came hurtling down toward their heads!

CHAPTER 6

A Lost Boy

THE Hollisters dodged, but the objects thrown from the bridge landed squarely on all of them.

Mud! Gobs of it!

"Ugh!" Ricky cried, wiping it from his eyes. The mud had splattered in their hair and run down their faces. Their clothes were ruined. Sue began to cry.

"Who could do such a mean trick!" Pam exclaimed angrily.

"I have an idea who did it," Pete announced, and raced up the side of the embankment to the road which went across the bridge.

He looked on the bridge. Nobody was there. Turning, the boy peered in the other direction. Somebody was just disappearing among the bushes at the side of the road.

Pete ran as fast as he could toward the spot. But when he reached it, the person was gone. A car came toward him, and Pete waved his hands for it to stop.

"Why, hello there," called a friendly voice.

"Oh Mr. Finder," Pete said, "did you see a boy running through the field over there?"

"Yes, I did. Only a few seconds ago a boy dashed from the shrubbery and ran that way."

By this time Mr. Finder had taken a good look at Pete. "Say, what happened to you? Did you fall in the mud?" he asked.

When Pete explained what had happened to the children, Mr. Finder said it was a mean trick.

"Have you any idea who the prankster was?" the man asked. "It must be some one who knows you're looking for Old Moe."

"I think it was Joey Brill," Pete replied. "He's the only one in town who tries to make us Hollisters unhappy. And I suppose he's heard we're looking for Moses Twigg on account of Bobby. He doesn't like Bobby."

Just then the other children came along the road. What a sight they were!

Pam had tried to wash the mud from Sue's hair, but it had smeared over her rosy cheeks. Holly's blue sun-suit was full of brown spots, and Ricky's shirt was caked with mud.

Mr. Finder offered to take them all home, and they readily accepted. Pete helped his sisters into the car, cautioning Sue to sit on the floor so as not to get any mud on the upholstery.

Pete sat in front, alongside Mr. Finder. After the car started, the banker said, "I forgot to tell you before why I'm so eager to find out about Moses Twigg."

"You did tell us about his money," Pete said.

"Yes, but I didn't tell you that it has been in the

bank for nineteen years. If it stays there one more year, I'm afraid he's going to lose it."

"Why?" Pete asked.

Mr. Finder explained that after money went unclaimed in a bank for twenty years, it was given to the state.

"You mean Bobby and his mother couldn't have it?" Pete exclaimed.

"I'm afraid not."

"Then we're going to have to find Moses Twigg in a hurry, aren't we?" Ricky called out.

"You're right, young man."

He pulled up to the curb in front of the Hollister house, and his passengers hopped out. They thanked him and hurried in to their mother.

Upon seeing them, she stared unbelievingly.

"My goodness, what happened to you?" she cried, thinking they had been injured.

"We're all right," Pam assured her. "Just dirty."

She quickly told the story about the mudthrower, saying they thought he was Joey Brill.

"He probably thinks he's very funny," Mrs. Hollister declared.

She went to work immediately to wash Sue's hair, while the other children took baths and changed their clothes.

At dinner that evening, there was plenty to talk about. Mr. Hollister laughed heartily as Ricky told how they had scrambled around Mr. Kent's office trying to catch the frog, the lizards and the snake.

"That reminds me of the time that your Uncle Russ and I caught a giant frog down by the swamp when we were about your age," said his father, chuckling.

"Tell us about it," said Holly, who loved to hear her father tell stories of his boyhood.

"We had a terrible time catching the frog in the first place," Mr. Hollister began. "We trailed him around the edge of the swamp for nearly an hour. Then I crept up quietly behind him. As I leaned down to grab the frog, I lost my balance and fell in the marsh. Your Uncle Russ had to pull me out by my feet, so I wouldn't lose the frog."

"And did you take him home?" Holly asked.

"Yes, but again I got in trouble. Aunt Emma was visiting us, and she didn't like frogs. I got an old

She went to work immediately on Sue's hair.

cookie jar with a hole in the lid and put some water in it. Then Uncle Russ dropped the frog in.

"We went down to the cellar to make a nice big cage for him. In a minute, we heard Aunt Emma scream. She had taken the lid off the jar, and the frog had jumped right over her head."

The children roared with laughter.

"Did your mother let you keep the frog?" asked Pam.

"No," replied her father with a chuckle. "Aunt Emma was so startled that Mother thought we'd better take the frog back to the swamp. I guess he was happier there anyway."

Pete told his father about their trip through the newspaper office and how Mr. Finder was trying to trace Moses Twigg, too.

"You've been doing some first-rate detecting today," Mr. Hollister praised them. "Keep up the good work!"

"Dad, would you drive us out to Mr. Gillis's farm?" Pete asked him. "I want to ask Bobby if he knows when his mother's coming back."

"How about phoning?" Mr. Hollister suggested.

As soon as Pete finished dessert, he hurried to the phone and called the farmhouse. He let the bell ring a long time, but there was no answer.

"Couldn't we go anyway?" Pete begged. "Maybe everyone's outdoors, and they don't hear the phone."

"All right," Mr. Hollister consented. "All aboard!"

The children went but were disappointed. Mr.

No one was at home.

Gillis, Mrs. Bindle and Bobby were not at home.

"Let's come again tomorrow," Pete suggested.

As they rode back through town, the Hollisters kept a sharp lookout for Bobby. Pam thought he might be going from door to door selling cookies. But they did not see the boy, and finally Mr. Hollister took them home.

Weary, the children tumbled into bed, but fell asleep thinking of Bobby and wondering where he was.

"I hope that mean farmer isn't making him—making him—" Pam was thinking drowsily.

The next thing she knew the morning sun was shining brightly. Holly awoke a few minutes later, and they dressed, all the while talking about what they would tell Bobby.

The family came down for breakfast. They were in the midst of their meal, when they heard loud talking but could not make out the words.

"Say, that's coming over a loudspeaker," Pete said. "Mother, will you excuse me while I go out and see what it is?"

Mrs. Hollister said her son might go if he would come right back. Pete got up and hurried outside. In a few moments, he returned.

"It's a loudspeaker, all right," Pete said. "It's on a police car coming down the street."

Hearing this, all the children asked to be excused and raced out of the house.

"Let's go down the street to meet it," Pam suggested.

As the Hollisters approached the slowly moving vehicle, they saw that it was driven by Cal Newberry. Officer Cal was a nice policeman who had helped the Hollisters solve their first mystery in Shoreham.

"What's he saying?" Sue demanded.

Every once in a while Cal would stop the car, put a microphone to his mouth and speak into it. As the children listened intently, they finally caught the words.

"Bobby Reed is missing. Bobby Reed is missing. Has anybody seen Bobby Reed?"

CHAPTER 7

A Dog Detective

WHEN the children heard that Bobby Reed was missing, they rushed up to Officer Cal. Stopping his car, the policeman told them that Bobby had not been seen since the previous morning. Mrs. Bindle and the police had looked everywhere but could not find him.

"Oh, poor Bobby!" Pam cried out. "Do you think he had an accident?"

"We hope not," the policeman replied.

Pete thought Bobby had run away because Mr. Gillis treated him so badly, and said so.

"Bobby Reed is missing!"

"That could be right, of course," Officer Cal nodded. "But I know Bobby pretty well, and I don't think he'd run away from trouble. He's a good sport."

"Yes, he is," Pam agreed. "And he likes Mrs. Bindle."

The policeman said he must leave now and continue his hunt for Bobby.

"We'll hunt, too," said Pete.

Officer Cal thought that this was a good idea, but wondered how the Hollisters could find the boy when the police had not been able to.

"We'll use Zip," Ricky said. "He's only a collie, but I'll bet he's as good as a bloodhound."

The policeman smiled. "Try it," he said and drove off.

Ricky gave a sharp whistle, and Zip bounded from around the side of the house. He stood before the children, his ears cocked, as if awaiting orders.

"You're going to be a Detective Dog," Holly said as she patted him.

After telling their parents what they wanted to do, the four older children discussed how to start their hunt.

"Let's go over to the farm first and give Zip the scent," Pete suggested.

Mr. Hollister drove them there and went to the door with them to see if there was any recent news of Bobby. When they knocked, Mrs. Bindle appeared. Her eyes were red from crying, and they knew the boy was still missing.

Zip picked up the scent.

"We've come to help find Bobby," Pete said. "Mrs. Bindle, this is my father."

"Good morning, Mr. Hollister," she said. "This is a dreadful state of affairs. Oh, how can I ever tell Mrs. Reed!"

"Don't give up hope," the children's father advised. "Probably Bobby will be back long before his mother arrives."

"Maybe our dog Zip can pick up the scent," Pam added. "Do you have some of Bobby's clothes that he can smell?"

Mrs. Bindle said it was very kind of the Hollisters to help in the search. She went to Bobby's room and returned with one of his sweaters and a shoe. Pete took it.

"Here, Zip," he said. "Smell this."

The dog seemed to know exactly what the children wanted. He sniffed at the sweater and the shoe.

"Now find him, boy!" Pete ordered.

The dog put his nose to the ground and went back and forth outside the door of the house.

"Hurrah, he has the trail!" Ricky yelled, as Zip set off in a straight line.

As Pete, Ricky and Holly followed him, Pam lingered behind to ask Mrs. Bindle a question.

"Did Bobby take any extra clothes with him?" she inquired.

The housekeeper said no. He had taken nothing but a loaf of bread. "That's what makes me think he planned to go fishing, maybe," the woman said. "Oh, I hope he's all right."

"I'm sure Bobby's perfectly safe," said Mr. Hol-

The collie led them to the river.

lister reassuringly. Then he left, as he had to keep a business appointment.

"We'll let you know if we find any trace of Bobby," Pam said to Mrs. Bindle, and ran after her sister and brothers.

Zip, meanwhile, kept sniffing the ground. After what Mrs. Bindle had said, Pam was surprised to see that the dog was heading straight to town and not the river. Finally Zip arrived in front of *The Trading Post* and stood still, sniffing just below the window.

"Bobby must have come here to look at the fish," Pete said.

"He wanted to win the prize so badly," Holly remarked, "that maybe he went off to find a big fish."

Suddenly Zip started off again with the four Hollisters following. He led them along a path toward the Muskong River bank. When they came to a railroad crossing, Zip stopped to sniff around for a few seconds.

"Maybe he stopped here hoping to get a ride on a train," Ricky surmised.

But Holly thought Bobby would have more sense than to try to jump on even a slow moving freight train. He might have sat down to rest a few minutes, or stopped to look up and down the tracks before he crossed.

In a few moments, Zip continued his search across the track and ran along the trail toward the Muskong River, keeping his nose close to the ground.

Finally the faithful collie led them to the river bank near the Stone Bridge. He went clear to the water's

edge, then stopped. The dog sniffed some more, looking inquiringly at the children. It was evident that he
had lost the scent at this point.

"Oh dear," Holly said, "I hope Bobby didn't fall
in and drown."

"Don't think such things," Pam shuddered.

Suddenly Pete shouted, "Look, the old rowboat is
gone! The one we tried to rescue."

The children gazed at the spot where the battered
old boat had rested in the mud.

"If Bobby tried to go fishing in that," Pete said,
worried, "I don't think he got far."

Fearful that the boy might have taken the old boat
down the river, the children searched the shore front
for some distance. Not seeing it, they sat down, wondering what to do next.

"We can't go out on the river alone," Pam sighed.
"Who can take us? Dad maybe?"

"No, he's going out of town today, I heard him
say," Pete spoke up. "Say, I know somebody, if he'll
do it."

"Who?"

"Bachelor Bill."

Bachelor Bill was a broad-shouldered, good-natured
man who spent most of his time outdoors. Once,
when Pete was pinch-hitting at *The Trading Post* for
an hour, he had sold the man a large canoe. His name
was William Barlow, but everyone in town called him
Bachelor Bill.

"Let's find out if he'll take us," Pam said eagerly.

The Hollisters hurried home. Pete quickly thumbed through the telephone book for the number and called Bill. Luckily, he was home.

When the boy told him about Bobby and asked if he would help them search for him, Bachelor Bill said he would start at once.

"But I can take only two of you," he added. "I'll meet you at the Stone Bridge in half an hour."

It was decided by Mrs. Hollister that Pete and Pam would go with Bill. Saying good-by, the children hurried back to the river bank. Not long after they reached it, they saw Bill in his canoe. He drew up to the river's edge and held the canoe securely as the two children stepped in.

"You paddle up front, Pete," Bill said. "I'll take the stern, and, Pam, suppose you sit in the bottom of the canoe and be our lookout."

Giving his paddle a good push against the shore, Bill sent the canoe skimming out over the river. They started downstream because Bill thought it was very unlikely that Bobby could have gone upstream in the old rowboat. It would have been almost impossible for a boy of his size to row against the current.

After a few minutes, they passed a small launch anchored near a bend in the river where the current was not so strong. Two men in the boat were fishing.

Pete called over to them, "Did you see a boy alone in a battered rowboat anywhere along this river?"

"No," came the answer.

"Did you see a boy in a battered rowboat?"

"Have you been here long?" Bill asked them.

"Since five this morning."

"Then Bobby passed here before that," Bill told the children. "That is, if he came at all."

Farther on, they passed a boat anchored near shore. A man in it was tinkering with his outboard motor. They asked him about Bobby.

"No," came the reply. "I've been fussing with this cantankerous motor most all morning, and I'd have seen if a boy had passed me."

They paddled on, beginning to feel discouraged. Whenever they saw a boat, they asked the occupants for news of Bobby. No one had seen him.

After a while they noticed a pretty sight ahead of them. Across the river stretched a line of toy sailboats.

"They're having a race," Pete said.

Pam had an idea. If Bobby had come this way recently, surely he would have stopped to watch the race.

"Let's see if he's here. If not, we'll ask the contestants if they've seen Bobby Reed," she proposed.

"All right," Bachelor Bill agreed.

They paddled over to a group of boys standing on the left bank of the river. They were cheering and waving their arms, as one boat, then another, took the lead in the race. Pam and Pete looked at the boys intently, hoping to see Bobby among them. He was not there.

Careful not to disturb the small sailboats, Bill steered the canoe up to the place where the boys were standing. Pete and Pam stepped onto the shore, and approached a young man who seemed to be in charge.

"Have you seen a boy named Bobby who might have come past here in an old rowboat?" Pete asked him.

The man had not noticed but said he would ask the boys. He questioned each of them. Finally a red-haired lad said:

"There was a kid here about a half hour ago. I don't know who he was. Never saw him before."

Pam was excited. "Was he about ten years old, and did he have brown eyes?" she asked.

"I didn't see the color of his eyes," the boy replied, "but he was about my size."

"They're having a race!"

"That might have been the boy we're looking for," Pete said. "Where did he go?"

"He watched the race a while and then went off in the woods that way." He pointed.

The Hollisters told Bill what they had learned and said they would like to search for Bobby in the woods.

"Will you wait here while we go look?" Pam asked the bachelor.

"All right, but don't go far."

Pete and Pam ran off in the direction the boy had indicated. As they went deeper among the trees and bushes, the children shouted:

"Bobby, Bobby, where are you?"

There was no reply. Presently they came to a small trail. Pam thought anyone going through this way would probably follow it. They hurried forward and continued their shouting. After they had gone some distance, Pete said:

"Listen! I hear something!"

At first Pam thought it was merely an echo, as she shouted Bobby's name again. But finally a feeble reply came back.

"Oh, do you suppose we've found him?" she cried excitedly, dashing forward with her brother. "Bobby, are you there?" she called.

"Here I am. What do you want?"

Pete and Pam dashed into a small clearing, where a boy was picking berries. His back was to them. He turned around.

"Does my mother want me?" he asked.

Pete and Pam stared in surprise. This was not Bobby Reed after all!

"Is your name Bobby?" Pam asked.

"That's right. But who are you? I don't think I know you," the boy said, putting down his basket of berries.

"No, you don't," Pete said. "My sister and I are looking for another Bobby. A Bobby Reed. Have you seen him?"

"No."

Pete and Pam were discouraged. As they started back toward the river bank, Pete said:

"That was a wild goose chase."

Reaching the canoe, they got in and reported their failure.

"Too bad," said Bachelor Bill. "But we'll look in more places."

They set off again, each of them thinking hard about where the missing boy might have gone. Finally Bill remarked:

"If Bobby did row the old boat, there is one person who might have seen him."

"Who's that?" both children asked at once.

"Hugh, the model maker."

The Hollisters had heard about Hugh. He had a place on the river bank, where he carved model boats, and sold them to visitors. He spent all day on the dock so he would see everyone who passed.

Soon Hugh's dock loomed up ahead of them. Bill steered the canoe alongside it, and the model maker stood up to greet them.

"Morning. Did you come to buy a model canoe?" Hugh asked.

"No," Bachelor Bill answered. "We're looking for a lost boy. We think he set out on the river in an old beat-up rowboat."

"Hm," said Hugh and sat down again. Evidently he was disappointed at not making a sale.

"Have you seen any little boy rowing down this way alone?" Pam asked him.

The model maker scratched his head. "Why, yes, I think I did, come to think of it."

The children were excited. "When?" they asked.

Hugh went on, "I saw a boy go past here in an old

"Did you come to buy a model canoe?"

boat yesterday noontime. The current was carrying him along, and he was bailing water out of the boat like fury. I don't see how the old tub stayed afloat."

"Oh, it was Bobby! I just know it was Bobby!" Pam said excitedly.

CHAPTER 8

Capsized!

"O<small>H</small>!" P<small>AM</small> cried out when she heard about the boy in the leaky rowboat.

"I'm sure he was Bobby!"

Pete and Bachelor Bill were worried about him too. There was no telling how long the lad could stay afloat, no matter how hard he bailed.

"Yup," Hugh, the model maker, continued. "I called to the boy, but he didn't answer. I'd loaned my canoe to a friend, so I couldn't go out to help him. He was still bailing out water when his boat disappeared around the bend in the river down there."

"Let's get going," Pete suggested.

He thanked Hugh for his information, then Bill sent the canoe speedily on its way. As he and the children scanned the shore line, Bill asked whether Bobby could swim. The Hollisters did not know. But Pam said that even if he could, she was fearful he could not reach the shore. The river was so wide at various points that a small boy could easily get tired and not be able to swim so far.

"Too bad he had such a head start on us," Bill said. "He could be anywhere by this time—even miles

Pam opened the basket to find their lunch.

down the river. And that's where I'm inclined to think he is; as far away from that mean farmer as he could get."

This remark encouraged Pete and Pam. Even when they asked two other people about the lost boy, and the answer was no, they did not feel so hopeless about him. Finally Bill looked at his wrist watch.

"We'd better not go any farther," he said. "It's going to take longer to paddle upstream back to Shoreham. Meantime, let's stop for some lunch."

"But we didn't bring any!" Pam exclaimed, her hand flying to her cheek in dismay.

Bill Barlow grinned and said not to worry. Reaching under the seat, he pulled out a flat picnic hamper and handed it to Pam. Then he guided the canoe to a clearing on the river bank. For the first time on the trip, looks of concern vanished from the faces of Pete and Pam.

"Thanks for packing the lunch," Pam said with a pretty smile. "You never forget a thing."

He gave her a big wink. "I don't forget I have a big appetite. I'll bet I can eat as much as you two!"

They all laughed as the canoe touched the shore.

"Here's a good spot," Bill said, "with an old fireplace, where we can roast what I brought."

Pete hopped out first and after the others stepped to the ground, pulled the canoe up. Pam opened the basket to find frankfurters, rolls and a thermos jug of milk.

Pete started a fire, and Pam roasted the frankfurters on long willow sticks that Bill had gathered.

All three were hungry from their long trip, and enjoyed the delicious picnic. When they finished, Pete took an old can from the canoe. He filled it with water and doused the fire. As Pam was picking up the scraps, she suddenly exclaimed:

"See what I found!" In her hand was a piece of wrapper from a loaf of bread.

Pete and Bill could not understand what was so exciting about a bread wrapper and asked her.

"It's from Miller's Bakery in our town!" Pam said. "Bobby took half a loaf of bread with him. Don't you remember Mrs. Bindle said so?"

Pete's eyes grew wide over this clue to the missing boy. "You mean maybe he stopped here?"

"Yes."

Bill agreed that this might be true, and said he was sorry not to continue the search. "Will you come back with us tomorrow?" Pete asked.

The bachelor replied that he couldn't. He had to go out of town. Maybe one of his friends could continue the search with them.

"I wish Uncle Russ were here with his boat," Pam sighed. Uncle Russ was the children's favorite uncle. He was jolly and always saying funny things. They loved to take rides on his boat.

"We haven't seen him in so long he must be on a trip," Pete remarked.

Pam put the bread wrapper in her pocket, and they returned to the canoe. When she and Pete were in their places, Bill put one foot into the canoe and shoved off with the other.

Once in midstream, he headed into the current, which was swift. The bachelor had strong arms, however, and Pete also had firm muscles. After they had paddled awhile, Pam glanced back and saw a motorboat coming upstream.

"Let's ask that man if he saw Bobby down the river," she suggested.

As the motorboat drew closer, Bill shouted, "Say, that's the *Beeline*. A friend of mine owns it."

The driver slackened speed as he drew abreast of the canoe, so the waves would not endanger the smaller craft. Bill waved his canoe paddle.

"Hello there, Henry!" he shouted. "Hold on a minute."

Henry throttled his motor down and came alongside the canoe. He was a slim young man about eighteen, with black wavy hair and glistening white teeth. He smiled broadly, saying he was glad to meet the Hollisters.

"Have you been way down the river?" Pam asked him.

"About ten miles."

"Did you see a boy in an old rowboat or hear anything about him? His name's Bobby Reed."

"I saw the police boat scouting along both shores," Henry replied. "A fellow said they were looking for a missing boy."

"He's the one, all right," Pete spoke up. "Oh, I hope they find him."

"I do too," said Henry. "Say, you folks are a long way from home. Want a lift?"

"That would be swell." Bill grinned.

Pam giggled at the idea of hitchhiking on a river, but it would be fun to ride on the speedy motorboat.

"I think there's room enough to lift the canoe aboard," Henry said, glancing at the deck of his boat. "But I've never given a canoe a pickaback before."

Pete snapped his fingers. "You might not have to. Why don't we tie the canoe to the back of your motorboat? Bill can ride with you. Pam and I'll stay in the canoe."

"Good," Henry agreed. "A river towboat." Bill thought about the idea a moment. "We'll have to tie

"Whee! This is like a toboggan!"

you on with a long rope," he said, "because the wake of the *Beeline* could easily upset you."

Henry said he had a long rope and reached into a locker for it. He fastened one end to a metal ring in the stern of the motorboat and then handed the other end to Bill. After the bachelor attached it firmly to the wooden bar near the bow of the canoe, he stepped into the motorboat.

"Have fun!" he called to the Hollisters.

Henry started the engine. The motorboat moved slowly, until the towline was taut. Then Henry gave her power and shot rapidly ahead.

Bill watched the children for a few minutes to be certain they were safe. Pete grinned and shouted that they were having a grand time, but Bill could not hear him because of the motor's roar. He turned back to talk to Henry.

"Whee!" Pete exclaimed. "This is like a water toboggan!"

The waves made by the motorboat slapped against the canoe sending up spray and soaking them.

"We ought to have our bathing suits on," Pam giggled.

"We'll get home in no time at all," Pete laughed.

As they sped past several other canoes, Pete and Pam waved. Several children called, "Take us along!"

The rest of what they said was lost in the wind.

"Holly and Ricky would love this," Pam thought as they raced toward Shoreham.

Pete glanced at the motorboat, where Bill and Henry sat with their backs toward the children. Suddenly the boy caught his breath. The rope was loosening from the boat inch by inch!

Pete shouted to Bill. But the man could not hear him because of the wind and the roar of the engine.

"Pam! Pam! Where are you?"

Pam now saw what was happening. She cupped her hands to her mouth and cried out too, but she could not make Bill or Henry hear her.

"What'll we do?" Pam shouted to Pete.

"Hang on tight!"

Pam fearfully clutched the sides of the canoe as the last bit of rope worked its way loose. Suddenly the canoe was adrift! It kept going forward twenty feet from the momentum, then stopped. It was caught in the backwash of the motorboat and spun around crazily. The next second it overturned. The brother and sister were hurled headlong into the river.

Pete's head bobbed to the surface first. "Pam! Pam!" he shouted. "Where are you?"

At that instant he saw his sister's hand reaching frantically above the water by the side of the capsized canoe.

"She's trapped underneath it!" Pete thought desperately.

CHAPTER 9

The Beeline

SWIMMING rapidly to the side of the canoe, Pete dived underneath it.

Pam had become entangled in the towrope!

Her brother quickly unwound it and gave her a push upward. Pam struggled to the surface of the water, reaching it just before her breath gave out. Pete followed her and helped Pam flop across the overturned canoe.

"Are you all right?" he asked anxiously.

"Y-yes. Thanks for saving me, Pete. I don't think I could have held out much longer."

With the anxiety for his sister over, Pete looked about for any signs of a rescue. He saw none but in the distance was Henry's motorboat.

"It's turning around!" he cried out gleefully. "They've seen us!"

In a few minutes, the men reached them and held out helping hands so the children could climb aboard.

"What happened to you two?" Bill asked, as he hauled Pam up.

"The rope came loose," she answered.

"Boy, what a scare you gave us!" Bill cried.

Pete said he would get the towline. He threw the rope onto the deck of the *Beeline*. Bill securely tied the canoe, then he and Pete righted it.

"I think you'd better make the rest of the trip with us," Henry said, laughing, and held out a hand to help Pete scramble aboard. "Come on!"

"Not until I find something that's very important," Pete replied.

He dived into the water and headed straight to the bottom. He came up for air two or three times, but kept on diving.

"What's he after?" Bill asked, puzzled.

At first Pam wondered what her brother was up to. She soon guessed the reason but said nothing until Pete returned to the surface with a grin of satisfaction on his face.

In one hand he had the picnic basket. The others laughed and the bachelor said:

"I see you remembered about my big appetite."

Pete handed the basket up to him. Then with one quick spring from the water, he lifted himself skillfully over the side of the motorboat and sat down to catch his breath.

"Nice work," said Henry admiringly.

He turned the boat about and went downstream several hundred yards to pick up the floating paddles. Then they set off again toward Shoreham.

"You two will catch cold in those wet clothes," Bill said presently to the Hollisters.

"I have the answer to that," Henry chuckled, mo-

Pete swam to the surface.

tioning toward the little cabin. "There are some dry cloths in there. Help yourselves."

Pam entered the cabin first. She was gone a few minutes, and returned in an outfit which caused roars of laughter. She wore a pair of long dungarees, which were rolled up, a man's white shirt and a round white sailor hat.

"Now you look like a real skipper," Bill told her. "Your turn next, Pete."

The boy went to the cabin and returned shortly afterward in a pair of large khaki shorts, pulled in with a belt that went around his waistline twice, and an old mackinaw that hung on him like a tent. Both children stood barefooted, laughing at each other's getups.

"Well, at least you're dry," Bill said, "thanks to Henry's extra supply of clothes."

They spread out their wet clothes in the hot sun, and, by the time the boat was outside Shoreham, the wind had blown them dry. Pete and Pam switched from their oversized duds. But they had to carry their soggy shoes. Thanking Henry and Bill, they stepped ashore.

It was five-thirty when they reached home. As the two walked up the driveway, Holly and Ricky dashed out to meet them.

"Did you find Bobby?"

"Why are you carrying your shoes?"

"Wait a second, and we'll tell you," Pam said, hurrying into the house.

Pete and Pam told the story of their day's adventure. Pete was praised for his heroic rescue and Pam for her clue to Bobby's journey.

"Dad will be pleased to hear what you both did," Mrs. Hollister said.

Holly stood there, beaming. Pam and Pete knew she was bursting to tell them something.

"What have you been doing, Holly?" Pam asked her.

"I went to see Mrs. Bindle," Holly replied. "She gave me a cookie and said that Bobby's mother is hurrying home. She'll arrive in a few days."

"The police must have told her he's missing," Pete spoke up.

"No doubt," his mother said.

It was already past the usual supper time when Mr. Hollister drove in from work. The children rushed out to greet him, throwing their arms about him.

"Pete saved Pam, and Holly got a cookie!" Sue shouted.

"They came home holding their shoes," Ricky chimed in.

All of this confused Mr. Hollister. "Wait a second," he said, grinning and holding up his hands. "One thing at a time, please."

When the children finished telling their stories, Mr. Hollister said that the surprises of the day were not finished yet.

"You mean we're going to have more 'ventures?" Sue exclaimed in excitement.

They spread out their wet clothes.

"Not exactly an adventure," their father replied. "But it will be an extra special surprise."

"Oh, I love s'prises," Sue went on. "I hope it's a lollipop."

While his children besieged him for a clue to the surprise, Mr. Hollister glanced at his wrist watch. He smiled and winked at his wife. When Pam saw this, she said:

"You know the secret too, don't you, Mother? Please tell us what it is."

Before Mrs. Hollister could reply, the doorbell rang. "I guess the surprise is here," she laughed.

"May I answer the bell?" Ricky asked. Mrs. Hollister excused him from the table. When the boy reached the door, he let out a whoop.

"It's Uncle Russ!" he shouted.

Into the dining room, and holding Ricky like a sack of potatoes under one arm, strode a tall, good-looking man. He was their father's younger brother, who lived in Crestwood with his wife, Marge, and their two children, Teddy and Jean.

What a fuss the Hollister children made over him! He grinned broadly as they flocked about.

"We heard how you put a frog in the cookie jar when you were a boy," Holly teased him.

"You did? And did you hear about the night your father went looking for our pet cat, and it turned out to be a skunk?" he asked.

The children loved Uncle Russ. Not only was he always full of jokes, but he could draw funny pic-

Uncle Russ grinned broadly.

tures. He was a cartoonist and drew comics for the newspapers. This was the reason the children always wanted to be first to see the paper every evening.

Mrs. Hollister invited Uncle Russ to have some supper, but he said he already had eaten.

Sue grabbed her uncle by the hand. "C'mon, Uncle Russ," she begged. "Let's do our upside down trick."

The tall man reached down, grabbed the little girl, and set her on his shoulders. As Sue giggled in delight, her uncle bent his head forward and somersaulted Sue to the floor.

"Again," she begged.

Uncle Russ repeated the stunt, then smoothed out his rumpled hair.

"Whew! You must be drinking a lot of milk, because you weigh a ton, Sue."

He put his hand into his pocket. "Everybody close his eyes," he ordered. The children did this. Then he said, "Ready!"

When they opened their eyes, they saw a handful of lollipops.

"Oh," Sue exclaimed. "My lollipop s'prise came true."

"Your Aunt Marge made these for you," Uncle Russ told them. "They're especially good."

"Oh, thank you!" everyone said.

"Mine is a red camel," said Holly, unwrapping hers.

"And I've got a green bear," Pam chimed in.

"This one looks like a pink rabbit," said Sue. She had already bitten off a corner, so it was hard to decide what the animal really was.

"I wish Aunt Marge would show us how to make these lollipops sometime," Mrs. Hollister spoke up.

"Maybe we could even start a business and sell lollipops," Ricky suggested.

The children crowded around Uncle Russ and began to ask questions all at once. They wanted to know what their cousins were doing and why their Uncle Russ had come to visit them.

Stretching out in an easy chair, the cartoonist said that his family was fine and that he had been on a business vacation. When Pete asked what this meant, his uncle explained:

94

"First I went to buy a new boat. I call it the *Sweetie Pie*."

"A new boat?" Pete exclaimed. "That's super! Is it here?"

"Yes. I'll show it to you all tomorrow."

"Swell."

"After I got the boat," Uncle Russ went on, "I made a long trip alone down the Muskong River to draw some pictures for my comics."

"Please, can we see them?" Pam asked.

"Sure. They're in my brief case on the hall table. Will you get it, Pam?"

She hurried off and brought the bulging brief case. Uncle Russ opened it and pulled out several sketches. How funny they were! Sue giggled and Holly

"Everybody close his eyes," he ordered.

laughed. One showed a dog holding a hoop, and a clown jumping through it. Another showed an elephant riding on the handle bars of a boy's bicycle. Ricky said they were the luckiest children in the world to see comics even before they appeared in the newspaper.

Suddenly Pam noticed a pencilled sketch on a larger piece of cardboard. It was a picture of a boy sitting on the river bank.

"Uncle Russ!" she exclaimed, as she stared at the drawing. "Who is this?"

"I don't know. Some little boy down the river," he answered.

"It looks just like Bobby Reed, a boy who's missing from Shoreham!" Pam said excitedly.

The other children crowded around her. They agreed it surely did look like Bobby.

Uncle Russ said the lad had been sitting quietly on the shore many miles below Shoreham. The little fellow had had such a sad expression that he had felt sorry for him. When he suddenly saw Uncle Russ, who had just finished the sketch, he had dashed off into the woods on the river bank.

"I'll bet he was Bobby Reed!" exclaimed Pete.

Suddenly Pam said to her uncle, "Will you please take us in your boat to find Bobby Reed?"

CHAPTER 10

A Tricky Machine

AFTER Uncle Russ had heard the whole story, he said, "I'd like to help you hunt for Bobby Reed, but I'm afraid there are complications."

"We'll eat the complicakes," Sue said eagerly.

Uncle Russ smiled. Picking up his little niece, he added, "I mean, there may be reasons why I can't go on the river trip with you."

"You mean your boat won't work?" Ricky asked.

"No, the *Sweetie Pie* is shipshape and ready for a long voyage," Uncle Russ replied. "The point is, I'm due back at my office with these cartoons."

Holly sighed. Twirling one of her pigtails, she declared sadly, "Maybe we'll never see Bobby Reed again. He may disappear just like his great-grandfather did."

The children's disappointment disturbed Uncle Russ. He put Sue down and said, "I'll telephone my office. I was going to leave tomorrow. But if I can stay for a few more days, I'll take you all on a river trip to help find little Bobby."

Holly, hopeful at once, jumped up and down and

clapped as Uncle Russ took the telephone and called long-distance.

"Won't it be wonderful," Pam said, "if we can take a ride down the river in the *Sweetie Pie?*"

"Maybe we can fish on the way," said Pete, who was always eager for a chance to catch more Muskong bass.

"And maybe I can find a lopadupalus for Mr. Kent," Ricky said gleefully.

When Uncle Russ said hello, the children instantly became quiet. As he spoke to someone in his office, they waited eagerly. But the reply from the other end of the line made him frown.

"Well, I guess you're right," he said. "Yes, I'll do that. Good-by."

He hung up the phone and turned to the children, shaking his head. "I can't take you," he said. "My office needs me. Emergency job waiting for me there. I'm terribly sorry."

Holly's lower lip began to tremble. She sniffed a couple of times and brushed her eyes with the back of her hand. The other children looked woebegone, too. Mr. and Mrs. Hollister were also sorry that Uncle Russ could not take his nephews and nieces on a rescue expedition down the river.

Sue looked up into Pam's face. "We can take our rowboat, can't we?" she asked. Pam did not answer but put her arms around her little sister.

Uncle Russ mopped his forehead with a handker-

Uncle Russ called long distance.

chief. Then suddenly he gave the children a big smile.

"I have an idea," he said.

"What?" they chorused.

"Maybe you can go on a river trip after all," he replied, "even if the police find Bobby."

"Yikes!" Ricky shouted. "How can we do it, Uncle Russ?"

As everyone brightened, their uncle grinned even more broadly. "Your dad can be the skipper of the *Sweetie Pie*," he said. "He can take you all on the trip, and I can go back home by train."

Mr. Hollister looked startled. "Hold on a minute, Russ," he said. "I also have business to attend to."

Mrs. Hollister laid a hand on her husband's arm. "Can't you get somebody to take care of *The Trading Post* for a few days?" she asked pleadingly.

"Yes, Daddy! Yes, Daddy!" the children cried together.

Mr. Hollister scratched his head and squinted one eye. "Well, I guess maybe it could be done."

"Tinker can mind the store!" Pete said enthusiastically.

"I believe he can," Mr. Hollister said. "He has enough experience to do it, but he'll need some extra help."

Pete snapped his fingers. "I've got it, Dad!" he said. "Dave Mead can help him. He's very bright and quick, and loves the store."

By now the children were so excited that they began to dance around their mother and father and Uncle Russ.

"I told you it would all work out," Uncle Russ said, smiling.

"Oh, this is so exciting," Mrs. Hollister exclaimed. "If Dave Mead helps Tinker at The Trading Post, we can start on our river trip tomorrow."

Mrs. Hollister's words were just like starting a race. Pete dashed out of the door to find Dave Mead.

"I want to take White Nose with me," Holly declared as she looked about for her pretty cat. "Donna Martin would just love to take care of the five kittens. They'd make too many to look after on the boat."

Pam had an idea too. "I think Jeff and Ann Hunter will be glad to take care of Zip and feed the fish in the tank at The Trading Post," she said. "I'll go now and ask them."

In a few minutes, there was not one Hollister child left in the house. They were all off on errands in preparation for the exciting trip.

While they were gone, Uncle Russ explained the workings of the *Sweetie Pie* to his brother. It was a thirty-three foot cabin cruiser which had been named by his daughter, Jean.

Uncle Russ had just finished telling his brother how the boat was operated, when his nieces and nephews came rushing back, all out of breath.

"Dave Mead will help Tinker!" Pete shouted.

Holly came into the living room, holding White Nose under her arm like a purse.

"Mother," she said, with her cute smile, "Donna will take care of our kittens. She's going to let them sleep in her doll house."

"That's fine," Mrs. Hollister said. Then with a wink at her husband, she added, "If you squeeze White Nose any harder, she won't have enough breath left to make the trip with us."

Holly put the cat down, and White Nose hopped onto her favorite spot in the corner of the sofa. The next moment Sue came in with her sand toys to take on the trip. Ricky followed with a jar to hold any frogs or strange fish he might capture on the river.

The next good news was that Ann and Jeff had agreed to keep Zip and feed the fish.

"Oh, boy!" Pete said. "Now we're all set to go."

"Not so fast," Mr. Hollister advised. "Don't forget we have to stock up on food for this trip."

Sue came in with her sand toys.

"And we have to look at the beautiful new boat, too," Mrs. Hollister said. "Do you suppose we can go down to see it now, Russ?" she asked.

When the children heard this, they clapped and begged to go.

"Okay," Uncle Russ said. "The *Sweetie Pie* is tied up at the Shoreham municipal docks. Let's take a look at her."

The children climbed hurriedly into the back of the station wagon. Zip sprang in, too. Soon they were on their way to the busy town dock. The children had been there before to look at the many trim boats which are anchored there.

"There she is," Uncle Russ told them.

"Say, isn't she a beauty?" Mr. Hollister exclaimed.

The *Sweetie Pie*, a beautiful white and mahogany craft, rocked gently in the water.

The Hollisters jumped out of the car, hurried to the edge of the dock and stepped down into the stern deck of the *Sweetie Pie*, which held several chairs.

"How much space there is!" Pam said gleefully. "The deck's as wide as my bedroom!"

Midway of the boat was the roofed cabin with windows all around. On the left side at the rear was the driver's seat, high enough so he could see across the cabin.

Ricky slipped into the seat and gave the wheel a couple of twists. "Hold on everybody!" he shouted. "I'm going to make a sharp turn!"

Uncle Russ laughed. "Oh, come on," he said. "Before you start off, you should see the rest of the boat."

He went through a small door near the driver's seat and down three steps. On the left was a cozy dinette and as they looked to the right, Holly exclaimed:

"Oh—what a darling little kitchen!"

"Glad you like it," said Uncle Russ. Then he added with a grin, "only now that you're going to be real sailors, call it the galley. That's the name for a kitchen on board ship."

"Mother, won't it be fun to work in here," Pam said excitedly, as she examined the stove, refrigerator and cabinets full of pretty dishes.

"Indeed it will," replied Mrs. Hollister.

"Now I'll show you a trick of magic," Uncle Russ said, pointing at the dinette. "Hokus pokus! Presto chango!" He folded down the table top and pulled out the cushions. Now it was a big double bed.

"Gee, that's neat!" Pete exclaimed. "Who's going to sleep here?"

"You, Dad and Ricky," Mrs. Hollister said.

"How about us girls?" Holly asked.

Uncle Russ winked and opened a little door toward the front of the boat. In it were two more bunks.

"Oh, goody!" Sue burst out and crawled onto one of them. It was covered with a pretty blue spread, with an anchor embroidered on it. "I'm going to sleep right away." She closed her eyes. But she had a big smile on her face and could not keep from giggling.

Her father tickled her ribs, and she jumped off the bunk. Uncle Russ led them back on deck. He

"I'm going to make a sharp turn!" Ricky shouted.

leaned over and pulled out a big steel ring in the floor.

"Oh look! A trapdoor!" Ricky shouted as a piece of the floor lifted up. He whistled as he saw the glistening engine below. "What a honey!" he cried.

"You'll get a good bit of speed out of this," Uncle Russ said with pride.

"Jeepers!" Pete exclaimed in admiration. "And what a powerful battery, too."

When Uncle Russ closed the trapdoor, Holly grabbed his hand and pointed to the roof of the cabin. "Why is that rowboat up there?" she asked. "Is it for children to play with?"

"No. That's not a toy," he replied. "That small rowboat is called a dinghy. It's used to take people ashore when there is no dock."

"That would be exciting," Ricky piped up. "Maybe we can ride in it on our trip."

Pam noticed a cabinet near the steering wheel and peeked into it. Inside were two flashlights and a first-aid kit.

"What big flashlights!" she exclaimed.

When Uncle Russ heard this, he chuckled. "There aren't any street lights on the river, and it gets mighty dark out here."

Pam smiled. "The first-aid kit is like the one we have at home," she remarked.

"All this extra equipment comes in handy at some time or other," her uncle added, "just like this big horn."

He pressed a button near the driver's seat and a

"Why is that rowboat up there?" she asked.

deep throated sound boomed out from on top of the cabin. The horn was fastened up there.

"Oh, boy!" Ricky exclaimed in wonderment. "May I blow it, Uncle Russ?"

"All right. But only once. It might scare people on the dock."

Ricky pressed hard and long on the button, and the horn made the loudest growling noise he had ever heard.

"That's super," Pete said, thrilled. "It sounds like a fog horn."

"We use it for that and also to warn other boats that we're coming," Uncle Russ explained.

He next pointed out the boat's lights, a red one on the left side and a green one on the right.

"Port and starboard," Uncle Russ said. "Port is left and starboard is right. We keep them on all night for safety's sake."

A couple of minutes later, while Pete was admiring the chrome fittings, he noticed that someone on the dock was whistling. It was Joey Brill.

"Hi!" Pete called. "What do you want?"

"Let me play ball with Zip while you're looking at the boat," Joey said.

"Not now," Pete answered. "Zip might jump into the river and then get Uncle Russ's boat all wet."

Joey scowled and walked away as the children scampered about the deck.

Suddenly everybody was startled by a great splash.

"What fell into the water?" Mrs. Hollister asked.

"Zip! He jumped in." Pete said. "Joey deliberately threw a ball for him to get."

"That awful boy!" Pam cried. "Now Zip's all wet!"

The Hollisters watched as the dog swam quickly and steadily toward the ball, which was about fifty feet out in the water. The faithful collie was just about to grab the ball in his mouth when a cry went up from the *Sweetie Pie*.

"Come back! Come back!" Pete shouted.

Not far away a speedboat was racing right toward Zip. The man at the wheel could not see the dog in the dusk.

Would Zip be able to get out of its way in time?

CHAPTER 11

A Gumball Surprise

"Zip! Look out!" the girls shouted.

"Don't hit him!" Ricky screamed at the driver of the speedboat. The children waved their hands frantically to warn him. The dog had grabbed the ball in his mouth and, still directly in the path of the onrushing boat, started toward shore. He surely would be hit if he was not seen in time.

Suddenly Sue shrieked as only four-year-old girls can. The man heard her. He glanced at the children,

Zip was safe!

"Hey! Get away!" the boy shouted.

who were pointing at Zip. Instantly he swerved his boat.

Zip was safe!

"Oh, good!" Pam cried.

Everyone sighed in relief.

But Joey Brill, who had not seemed worried, was grinning because Zip was bringing him the ball.

"You almost made Zip get hit!" Holly called to him.

"I did not," Joey replied. "Your dog didn't have to chase my ball."

"You knew Zip would go after it if you threw it into the water," Pete declared hotly.

"So what!" Joey shouted. "He ought to be smart enough to get out of a boat's way."

"Who is this boy?" Uncle Russ asked, frowning. "He's certainly a trouble maker."

"He sure is," Ricky agreed.

He told his uncle about how Joey Brill was always pestering the Hollisters, as well as being a nuisance around the town.

"He took cookies away from Bobby Reed, too," Sue spoke up.

By this time Zip had reached the shore with the ball still in his mouth. He dropped it at Joey's feet. Then, as the boy bent over to pick it up, Zip shook himself vigorously. The muddy water from his long coat splashed over Joey's face and clean white shirt.

"Hey! Get away!" the boy shouted. "You're getting me all wet!"

Instead of running away, Zip only shook himself harder, and Joey's light colored pants were covered with brown spots. The Hollister children could not keep from giggling.

"Serves him right," said Ricky under his breath.

"I'll get even with you for this—you and your fresh dog!" Joey shouted.

He backed off a short distance, then leaned down and picked up a heavy stick.

"Don't you dare throw that stick at my dog!" Pam cried out, and started to run off the boat to rescue her pet.

Mr. Hollister called to Joey firmly, "You'd better not throw that, Joey."

The boy paid no attention. He was just about to

pitch the stick when a police car drove up to the dock.

"The cop'll get you, Joey!" Ricky yelled.

In the car was Officer Cal. Before he could get out, Joey gave one look, dropped the stick and raced off.

Officer Cal stepped from the car, waved to the Hollisters, then went inside the office of the municipal dock. Pete decided to run ashore to ask the policeman if he had heard anything about Bobby Reed.

"No, nothing new to report," the officer answered, so Pete told him about the boy his uncle had seen.

"Then we ought to have some word of Bobby in a day or two," Cal said. "I'll report what you've told me."

Pete related to the friendly officer their plans for a trip down the Muskong River in Uncle Russ's boat.

"We're going to hunt for Bobby, too," he said.

"Let's make a race of it," the officer suggested.

"Okay," Pete agreed, as Cal got into his car. "Only you have a head start."

"So if you win, that'll be an even bigger feather in your cap," the policeman replied, grinning.

After he had gone, the children played around the deck of the *Sweetie Pie*. Presently Uncle Russ went into the cabin and returned with a map and a chart of the Muskong River.

"You'd better study these, John," he said to his brother. "This chart shows the channels of the river and the spots where there are hidden rocks."

After Mr. Hollister had looked at the chart a few minutes, he said, "I think it would be a good idea for me to take these home and really study them tonight. Perhaps I can teach Pete to be the ship's navigator tomorrow."

"That would be fine," said his wife. "But right now I think we had better stock up on some provisions for our trip before it gets any later."

"Good idea," her husband replied.

"There's a super-market open tonight, Mother," Pam said. "We can get there before it closes."

Uncle Russ locked up the boat, then the Hollisters hurried to the station wagon. They soon arrived at the super-market. How the children loved to shop there!

"We'll need a lot of food. You'd better get two baskets," Mrs. Hollister said, so the children wheeled two shiny shopping carriages from a pile that was stacked nearby.

Sue looked up at Pete. "Will you give me a ride, please?" she asked. "I'm tired."

"Sure."

Pete leaned down, picked up his little sister and put her into a basket carrier. Then they all started on a tour of the super-market. Mr. Hollister picked up cartons of soda, while Mrs. Hollister and the children got meat, frozen vegetables, and lots of canned goods and fruit.

"Oh, this is going to be a wonderful trip," Holly exclaimed gleefully. "Mother, may we buy some candy, too?"

Mrs. Hollister said each one might pick out two

"Oh, this is going to be a wonderful trip."

bars. What fun it was selecting the candy in the shiny wrappers!

As the food shopping progressed, Ricky became tired of it and asked Uncle Russ to walk with him to the section where children's books and toys were sold. They went off and together looked them over. Then Uncle Russ said:

"Let's you and I plan a little surprise. We'll buy a few things, and you can hide them around the boat."

"You mean for a treasure hunt?" Ricky asked. "That's super."

They decided on two tiny dolls, a whistle and a midget fire engine.

"I suppose I can't hide one for myself," Ricky remarked wistfully.

"Well no," Uncle Russ replied, "but how about picking out your own prize right now?"

Ricky had spied a gum-ball machine near the toys. He loved gum and decided on a handful of these.

Uncle Russ gave him ten pennies. Ricky put one into the machine, pressed the lever and a black ball dropped out into the cup.

Ricky popped the gum into his mouth and put another penny into the machine. But this time no gum dropped out.

"I guess it's stuck," he said and reached his finger up inside the slot.

A moment later a scared look came over the boy's face.

"Uncle Russ, I—I can't get my finger out!" he wailed.

His uncle rushed to his side and tried to help. But the finger was wedged tightly and every time Ricky tried to pull it out, he cried in pain.

"W—what'll I do?" he asked, tears in his eyes.

A crowd had begun to gather, and several people offered advice, like "Put some oil on it," "Shake the machine, something's stuck." Uncle Russ had a different idea and asked a clerk where the manager was.

"He's coming this way now," was the reply.

When the manager arrived, Uncle Russ said they would have to take the machine apart so Ricky could get his finger out.

"Have you a screw driver handy?" Uncle Russ asked.

"Yes, I have."

The man went behind a counter and found a screw driver and also a wedge, which he handed to Uncle Russ. Between them they got the front of the machine off, and suddenly Ricky began to laugh. There he stood holding the shiny metal front with his left hand and one finger of his right hand still poked through it.

"You do look kind of silly," said a voice behind him. It was Holly, who had seen the crowd and come over. "What happened, Ricky?"

He told her, while Uncle Russ opened a snap lock and released the boy's finger.

"Oh, that feels better," Ricky said. "Thanks, Uncle Russ."

The manager was tinkering with the machine. He

"I—I can't get my finger out!"

finally got it working. Then he handed Ricky two handfuls of gum, saying:

"With my compliments, Sonny. Sorry you got your finger pinched."

"Well," said Ricky, eyeing the gum, "I guess it was worth it."

The other Hollisters had already gone out to the car with the packages. When Ricky told them what had happened, Pete said he was sorry not to have seen his brother holding up the gum machine.

"And I'm glad we didn't have to leave you stuck in the machine while the rest of us went on the river trip," his father teased.

In a short time he had driven back to the dock. The food was carried into the little galley and put away.

"Now we're all set for the trip," Mr. Hollister said. "I'll go over the river chart tonight and we'll be down here first thing in the morning."

The children were up early the next day. Directly after breakfast, Uncle Russ said good-by and wished them well.

"And I do hope you find Bobby," he added. "Let me know."

"We will."

Mr. Hunter, the father of Ann and Jeff, offered to ride with the Hollisters to the boat and drive the station wagon back to their garage.

How excited everyone was! Even White Nose meowed continually as Holly carried her to the *Sweetie Pie.*

"Don't you want to go?" Holly asked her.

"Maybe she misses her babies," Sue spoke up. She patted the cat. "Don't worry. We'll be back soon."

"Did anyone check the gasoline gauge?" asked Mr. Hollister.

"I'll do it," said Pete.

He stepped over to the dashboard of the cruiser to look at it.

"It registers full, Skipper," the boy reported to his father.

"Very good, Seaman Pete," said Mr. Hollister, grinning.

As they were about to cast off, Officer Cal came alongside. He said Bobby Reed had not been located yet.

"Good luck to you!" he called, as he started off.

"All my crew in their places?" Mr. Hollister called.

"Aye, aye, sir! Aye, aye, sir!" came the giggling replies.

"Then let's shove off," Mr. Hollister said, his eyes twinkling.

He pressed the starter. Nothing happened. He pressed it again.

The children looked at one another. What was the matter? The *Sweetie Pie* would not start!

CHAPTER 12

Treasure Hunt

WHAT could be wrong with the *Sweetie Pie?* Was the boat broken?

"Hm," Mr. Hollister said, frowning. "Russ told me this was in perfect running order."

He jumped up and opened the section of deck ahead of him that covered the motor. He tapped various gadgets.

"Everything looks all right," he said.

Meanwhile Pete had started to check the wires. He finally came to the battery.

"I think I have it, Dad!" he exclaimed. "A cable leading to the battery is loose."

His father looked. "Sure enough."

Pete ran to the tool box which was in a locker in the galley, and returned with a pair of pliers. With nimble fingers he attached the cable and tightened the bolts that held it.

"Good job, son. Now I'll try the starter again," his father said.

As the others waited anxiously, Mr. Hollister pressed the button. The motor of the *Sweetie Pie* roared to life!

"Hurray, hurray!" Ricky shouted, and broad grins now replaced the anxious looks of the others.

"We're off!" Holly said gleefully as the propeller began to churn the water.

"Ship ahoy!" called Sue and the others laughed. "Good-by, Shoreham!" She waved.

The cruiser pulled away toward the center of the river.

"May I take the wheel when we get into midstream?" Pete asked.

"After a while. First you'd better study this chart carefully so that you'll know where the channel is. This boat draws a lot more water than a small motorboat. We don't want to hit a rock or become mired on a hidden mud bank."

"I'll say not," Pete grinned.

He spread out the chart and noted the curve of the channel, and location of shallow spots to be avoided. Finally, he declared he was ready to be the helmsman.

"Okay, son."

Mr. Hollister turned the wheel over to him. Pete guided the *Sweetie Pie* expertly, glancing at the chart in front of him every few minutes.

All this time Ricky had been very busy. For a while, he watched the scenery and the water. He especially liked the way the sunlighted backwash turned into every color of the rainbow as they rushed on.

Finally he decided to hide the little gifts he had bought the evening before. When this was done, he

"The pirate's treasure hunt is ready."

looked through the galley until he found two pieces of black cloth. One of these he attached to the small flag-pole at the stern. The other he wound around his head. Then in a loud voice he announced:

"The pirate's treasure hunt is ready!"

The others stared and then laughed.

"What's the treasure? Chewing gum?" Holly teased him.

"Better'n that," said Pirate Ricky.

Mr. Hollister took the wheel and the search started. Since Ricky could not join in, he decided to chew his own gift. Whenever anyone came near his treasure, Ricky chewed his gum furiously.

"Oh, ho!" Pete laughed as he reached under the overturned rowboat. "I have a doll to play with."

"That's for Sue," Ricky declared, so Pete handed it over, but he dropped out of the game.

It was not long before Sue found the midget fire engine under the life preservers in a locker. She gave it to Pete.

Holly spied her other doll among the canned goods, and Pam after a long search located the whistle under the mattress of her bunk.

"That was swell of you and Uncle Russ, Ricky," Pete said as he went back to take the wheel.

The girls played with their dolls, but Pam decided just to sit quietly in the bow with Pete and Mr. Hollister and look for any signs of Bobby Reed. In a little while they approached the place where she had found the bread wrapper. A man was fishing there.

"Can we stop here, Dad, and speak to that fisherman? He may have a clue," Pam said excitedly. "Bobby might have told him where he's going."

"That's a good idea," her father nodded.

He consulted the chart, then said they would not dare take the *Sweetie Pie* out of the channel at this point.

"We'll lower the rowboat, and you go talk to him," he said. "Mother can ride with you. I'll stay here."

Pete turned off the engine, and the others were told the plan.

It was quite a trick to lower the rowboat without hitting the sides of the cruiser, but finally they managed this. Mrs. Hollister got in first, and the oars were handed down to her. Then the two children jumped in, and Pete rowed them to shore.

"Hi, folks! You in trouble?" the fisherman called as they approached.

"Well, not exactly," Pete replied. "We're looking for a boy named Bobby Reed. Have you seen him?"

"Not that I know of," the man replied. "But a lad stopped here one day in the worst old fishin' boat I ever did see. Maybe that was Bobby."

"Did he say where he was going?" Pam asked excitedly.

"Not to any special place, mind you," the man said. "That lad just told me he was going after the biggest bass in the Muskong River."

Pete whistled. "Pam! Mother! That's it!" he cried.

Mrs. Hollister got in first.

"Bobby wants to win *The Trading Post* prize!"

"That still doesn't find him," Mrs. Hollister said.

The fisherman was sorry he could not help them more. As they were leaving he handed them a good-sized bass, saying he was having fine luck and would they like it for their lunch.

"Indeed we will, and thank you so much," Mrs. Hollister said, laying the fish in the bottom of the rowboat.

When she and the two children were once more on the *Sweetie Pie* and the rowboat hoisted aboard, Pam told the others of the new clue.

"Let's ask every fisherman we meet about Bobby," Holly suggested.

But as the day wore on none of the fishermen they asked had even caught a glimpse of the missing boy. They themselves saw no sign of Bobby or his boat.

"I think we had better stop for the night soon," said Mr. Hollister, who was at the wheel.

By looking at the chart, he found a sheltered cove where the water was free of rocks and deep enough for the *Sweetie Pie,* but out of the line of river travel. He steered into it and turned off the engine. The anchor was dropped.

"May we go for a swim before dinner?" Ricky asked his mother.

"Why yes, dear."

All the Hollisters put on their bathing suits, and a life jacket was strapped onto Sue. Soon everyone was swimming and splashing in the water.

Pete dived into the water.

Pete, Pam, Ricky and Holly climbed again and again onto the stern of the launch and dived into the water. Suddenly Pete cried out after Ricky went under and did not come up:

"Something's happened to him!"

He dived under the water to look around while the others called the boy's name. Suddenly a voice piped up:

"Here I am! On the other side of the boat. I swam under."

"Well, I'm thankful you're all right," Mrs. Hollister called, "but don't scare us that way again."

And his father warned him not to do this any more because he might hurt himself by hitting the propeller, even though it was not going around.

"All aboard!" Mrs. Hollister called presently.

Everyone climbed aboard and dressed. Then they sat down to dinner.

"This is just like one big picnic, isn't it?" Holly exclaimed as they ate a delicious supper of meatballs, potatoes and peas with ice cream and bananas for dessert.

While Mrs. Hollister helped the three younger children get to bed, Pam washed the dishes and cleaned up the galley. How she made the pots and pans shine!

Pete meanwhile was on deck trying out his fishing line, while Mr. Hollister sat on one of the cushioned seats watching. It was growing dark and Pete was just about to give up when suddenly there was a strong tug on his line.

"I've got something, Dad!" he exclaimed in excitement.

The fish gave Pete a tussle, but he finally reeled it in.

"A Clown Fish. A big one, too," his father said.

"And look, here's a tag!" Pete exclaimed. "It reads 'Old Moe 69'. Dad, maybe we're getting near the place where Old Moe lives!"

Mr. Hollister was as excited about this as Pete. They might be nearing the solution of the mystery of the tagged Clown Fish!

As Pete took the hook out of the fish's mouth, he noticed a waving light on the opposite shore.

"Look at that, Dad! You don't think Old Moe could be signaling?"

Mr. Hollister glanced toward the shore. Someone with a flashlight began to signal SOS.

"Somebody's in trouble!" Mr. Hollister said, recognizing the code. "I think we'd better go over there and find out what's the matter. Go tell Mother."

Pete went to tell her, then got the first-aid kit. His father was already putting the rowboat over the side. Pam came on deck.

"Please let me go," she begged.

"All right," her father agreed.

The three set out for the far shore. When the boat touched the gravelly shore, the Hollisters jumped out. A boy ran up, saying excitedly:

"I've got something, Dad!"

"Will you please help us?"

"Of course. What's the trouble?" Mr. Hollister asked.

"One of the boys got cut."

The speaker, who said his name was Michael, led Pete, Pam and their father a short way into the woods, where six boys sat around a campfire. One of them lay on a blanket, his leg bleeding, though someone had put a tourniquet on it.

"Jack cut his ankle with an axe," Michael said, "and we've done all we could without a first-aid kit."

Pete brought out the Hollisters' kit and his father got to work, assisted by his children. They applied antiseptic to the wound and bandaged the boy's leg.

When they learned the boys had been camping and hiking for several days, Pam asked them if they had come upon Bobby Reed. But none of them had seen the missing child.

"We didn't see anyone but a strange old man," Michael spoke up. "Real old."

The Hollisters were interested at once. "What was his name?" Pete asked quickly.

"He didn't tell us. He just chased us."

"Why?"

"We don't know. But we think he had some secret he didn't want us to find out," Michael replied.

"Where was he?" Pam asked excitedly.

"Oh, miles down the river, in a very overgrown place. You can hardly see his cabin."

They bandaged the boy's leg.

"I'll bet he's Old Moe," Pete declared. The boys had never heard of him.

"Well," said Mr. Hollister, "if you fellows are all right, we'll go back to our boat."

"I'll be okay," said the lad with the injured ankle. "Thanks a lot, folks."

"Glad to help you."

The Hollisters set off toward shore. When they stepped into their boat and looked out over the water, they noticed that a fog was rising, ghostlike, from the river.

"We'd better hurry before this mist gets any thicker," Mr. Hollister said, as he used an oar to push the boat into deeper water.

But as he rowed toward the other shore, the fog

became thicker. It settled down over them like a fluffy blanket. The farther they got out, the denser it became until they could not see a thing.

"It seems as if we're right in the middle of a cloud," Pam said. "Do you suppose it will pass away, Dad?"

Her father replied that a breeze might blow the fog away but right now not a breath of air was stirring.

"Let's head back to the shore," Pete suggested. "It wasn't so soupy there."

Mr. Hollister and Pam agreed that this was a good plan. As their father bent to the oars, Pete called out, "Stroke, stroke!" just as if he were in a racing boat.

"We ought to be near shore by now," Pam remarked, as Mr. Hollister stopped rowing and looked about.

But the mist swirled even thicker around them.

"How are we ever going to find the *Sweetie Pie?*" Pam asked fearfully.

CHAPTER 13

A Boat in Trouble

A FRIGHTENING thought came to Pete, Pam and their father. They were lost in the river fog!

The boy whipped out his flashlight, but its beam could not penetrate the white mist which had settled in about them.

"Maybe the current will carry us far down the river," Pam worried. "Mother won't know what happened to us."

"What worries me is that we may be run down by another boat," Mr. Hollister said.

"I'll shout," Pete offered, as his father kept on rowing. "Ahoy, ahoy!" he called hopefully.

No one answered.

"Our only hope," Mr. Hollister said, "is that when mother sees the fog, she will realize what is happening and blow our horn."

He had barely uttered these words, when the *Sweetie Pie's* horn sounded in the distance.

Broomp, broomp, broomp it kept repeating.

"Thank goodness," Mr. Hollister sighed and rowed faster. "All we have to do now is to go toward that sound." But a few minutes later he added, "That's not going to be easy, though."

The horn kept blowing but the sound seemed as far away as ever.

"I think we're going in the wrong direction, Dad," Pam warned.

"I guess you're right," her father agreed. He pulled stronger on his left oar. "There, let's hope we're traveling directly toward the *Sweetie Pie*."

He kept rowing, and the sound of the horn gradually grew stronger.

"We must be nearly there," Pete said gleefully, but five minutes later he cried, "Dad, we're getting farther away from it again!"

Mr. Hollister changed his direction once more. But they seemed to draw very close to the fog horn and then suddenly be farther away from it again!

"Let Pete and me take the oars for a while," Pam said finally. "You need a rest, Dad."

Their father thought this would be a good idea, so he carefully changed seats with his son and daughter. Pete and Pam pulled evenly, and the boat sped across the foggy water. But they also had the same trouble their father had had, never seeming to get very close to the sound of the horn.

"Know what I think is happening?" Pam exclaimed.

"What?" Pete asked, perplexed.

"I think we're going in circles, just like hikers do when they're lost in the woods."

"I think we're going in circles."

"That's probably the answer," her father agreed. "Do you have a compass in your pocket, Pete?"

The boy said no. He had brought one from home but had left it in his bunk.

Suddenly the three were startled by a scraping sound on the bottom of the boat.

"We're grounded!" Pete shouted. "But we don't know where."

"I have an idea," Pam said. "If we're on the same side of the river as those boys are, we can call to them."

"What for?" Pete wanted to know.

"They're hikers, aren't they?"

"Sure."

"Then they'll probably have a compass. Maybe even one to spare."

"You're a whiz, Sis," Pete said admiringly.

Mr. Hollister chuckled. "I think, Pete, that you and I are a couple of dodos for not figuring that out ourselves."

They beached the boat and climbed onto the shore. It was exactly the same spot as where they had landed before. Pete and Pam shouted for the campers as loudly as they could.

A few moments later came answering cries, which soon were followed by footsteps. Michael stepped forward, beaming a flashlight.

"Somebody lost?" he asked. Upon recognizing the Hollisters, he added, "We thought you'd gone."

"We went in a circle and came right back here," Pete grinned and told how they had been confused by the fog.

"Have you a compass we could borrow?"

Pete and Pam shouted for the campers.

"I sure have." Michael reached into his pocket. "Here's one you may keep. It's old, but works well. Has a luminous face, too."

Pete took the compass and thanked the boy. Mr. Hollister picked up the oars and set off. As he rowed, Pete held the compass in the palm of his right hand.

"I've taken a bearing on the fog horn," he said, speaking like a true sailor. "Due west from here."

Pete guided his father expertly. "Left oar, right oar," he called out whenever the rowboat was getting off course.

"We're pretty close to home now," the boy said happily twenty minutes later.

"It sounds as though we're right on top of the *Sweetie Pie,*" Pam added, putting her hands over her ears.

Just then there was a hard bump, which threw the children forward.

"John—Pam—Pete!" Mrs. Hollister's anxious voice cried out from the deck of the cruiser.

"Hello, Mother!" Pam exclaimed. "We're back safe and sound!"

They threw the rowboat's rope up to her. She held it as they scrambled aboard.

"Whew!" Mr. Hollister exclaimed, as they started hoisting the rowboat to the deck, "I thought we'd never make it, Elaine."

Ricky, who was still up, listened wide-eyed at the story of their adventure.

"Say, that's a neat compass," he commented.

"I thought we'd never make it!"

"I'm glad you were able to fix up that boy's ankle," Mrs. Hollister said.

"We got a good clue to Old Moe from Michael," Pete said. "They saw a strange old man who was hiding something."

"Not Bobby!" Mrs. Hollister exclaimed.

"Maybe he's helping Bobby get a big fish," Pam said excitedly.

"That reminds me," Mrs. Hollister said. "I have some news too. While you were gone, I was listening to the radio. The police report that Bobby has not been located yet."

"Then we have to find that old man," Pam declared.

"And that's not all," her mother went on. "According to the broadcast, Mrs. Reed has returned and is beside herself with worry about Bobby. She is begging everyone to hunt for her son."

"If Old Moe's got him, we'll just make him give him up," Ricky threatened.

"You've forgotten, dear," said his mother, "that we had an idea Old Moe might be Bobby's great-grand-father. Surely he'd send him home."

"That's right," Ricky sighed.

The mystery was too much for all of them, and Mrs. Hollister said that maybe after a good night's sleep they could figure things out better and find both Bobby and Old Moe.

When the sun came over the treetops on the shore of the Muskong River, the Hollisters made ready to continue their journey. The fog of the night before had been blown off by a stiff east wind and everyone was eager to continue the search. They had breakfast, then Pete helped his father pull up the anchor.

As they traveled down the river, the wind became stronger. Sue and Holly were asked to stay inside.

"It's too breezy on deck," their mother remarked.

"Let's play house in the galley," Holly suggested and the two little girls went off.

The wind became so strong that it whipped up whitecaps and froth on the surface of the river.

"Wow! This is a real blow!" Pete exclaimed, as he watched his father work hard to keep the cruiser on a straight course.

"I'd say it was a near hurricane," Mr. Hollister re-

136

"Look up ahead, Dad!" Pete warned.

marked, as he gazed at the gray sky which was quickly obscuring the sun.

The Sweetie Pie was being blown close to shore on their right despite all his efforts to keep it in the channel.

"It's a good thing there aren't any submerged rocks in this part of the river," he told Pete.

"Yes, but look up ahead, Dad," his son warned. "The place is full of tall weeds."

Mr. Hollister yanked on the wheel with all his might to avoid them but the Sweetie Pie merely plowed ahead.

"The wind's stronger than I am," he admitted, a worried look on his face. "But I don't dare stop."

As he said this, a tremendous gust of wind sent the

cruiser directly among the thick weeds. A few seconds later the *Sweetie Pie* stopped moving, its engine racing. Mr. Hollister immediately reduced the speed of the motor.

"We'll have to work out of this slowly," he told Pete.

"How, Dad?"

"By making our boat go backward and forward."

"Like getting a car out of a snowdrift?"

"Right."

Mr. Hollister put the motor in reverse for a few seconds, then started it forward. The *Sweetie Pie* gained a few feet every time he did this.

"We're going to make it!" Pete shouted, as the boat slowly crept through the clutching weeds.

But suddenly the motor started to groan. Mr. Hollister looked tense as he worked the throttle.

"I—I think—" he started to say, when the craft gave a little shudder and the motor stopped.

"We've stalled!" Pete cried.

"Our propeller must be fouled up in the weeds," his father declared. "Now we are in trouble."

CHAPTER 14

A Drifting Clue

"Pete and I can get those weeds off the propeller," Ricky said courageously. "We can dive under the boat and pull 'em."

"That's very fine of you to offer," said his father. "But I guess you don't realize how tough weeds are."

"No one may go overboard until it's calm," Mrs. Hollister said firmly, and her husband agreed.

In about an hour, the wind died down, and the sun was beginning to come out once more. Everyone trooped to the deck, except Pete and Ricky, who stayed below to change into their bathing trunks. When they appeared, Ricky asked:

"May we go after the weeds now?"

Mr. Hollister looked into the water. It was very clear and deep enough so the boys could not get stuck in the mud.

"Okay," their father said, "only wait for me. There's a lot of work to do."

He explained that not only would the weeds have to be removed from the propeller but a path would have to be made for the boat to get out. Otherwise, they would be fouled up again. He was ready in a jiffy.

"Here we go!" he said, and the three dropped overboard.

Pete, who went under first, popped his head up to report that the propeller was bound tightly by the weeds, and asked Pam to get his penknife. She returned with it shortly. Pete dived below again, with Ricky right behind him to help. The brothers kept bobbing to the surface for air and going down again.

"We nearly have the job finished," Ricky called up proudly a few minutes later. "A couple more dives and we'll be through."

Meanwhile, Mr. Hollister was swimming around with his own stout jackknife in one hand. He would dive under, hold a bunch of weeds in the other hand and cut them off cleanly. Gradually he was making a path for the *Sweetie Pie*.

Sue watched for a few minutes, then grew tired of it. She went to get some doll clothes she had washed and soon came back with a string and some tiny clothespins. At this moment, the two boys came to the top of the water, saying they had finished.

As Sue glanced down at them, she caught her breath. A large snake was swimming toward her brothers! As it wriggled along the top of the water, Sue shrieked.

"Pete! Ricky! A snake!"

The boys looked around them in the water, but from where they were they could not see the snake approaching.

"Where is it?" Pete wanted to know.

"There, right in back of you!" Holly burst out.

Still the boys could not find it. Seeing this, Sue threw the clothespins at the snake. It turned sideways, giving Pete and Ricky time to climb aboard.

Pete gave Sue a big hug. "Gee, I'm glad you saw that ugly creature. You saved us from being bitten!" he exclaimed.

"It might have been a water moccasin, and they're deadly poisonous, you know," added Ricky who had learned about snakes at school.

He and Pete waited for some time to make sure the snake was nowhere around, then they jumped back into the water to get the doll's clothespins. Sue watched carefully from the deck to make sure the snake did not reappear.

By the time they finished, Mr. Hollister was ready. The three swimmers dressed, then he pressed the starter button and the motor caught hold. Away they went toward the center of the stream.

"Oh look!" cried Holly, seeing a man's straw hat riding along on the current.

They whizzed by a lot of driftwood and two crates of oranges.

Holly started to giggle. "Oh, isn't that funny?" she exclaimed, pointing far out over the water.

On a large floating tree branch sat a hen holding her head up proudly. *Cluck cluck* she cried as they swept past her.

"Hi, skipper!" Pete shouted. "Come on aboard!" But the hen did not move.

Cluck, cluck she cried as she swept past.

"Maybe the chickie is setting out to seek her fortune," Holly said, thinking of fairy tales she had read.

"Oh, the poor thing," Pam remarked. "I do hope she lands safely."

Soon after Pam said this, a swirling eddy turned the piece of wood around and around.

"She may get dizzy and fall off," Holly worried.

But the wood stopped spinning and headed toward shore. As the children shouted encouragement to the hen, the wood touched the shore and she flew safely onto the river bank.

Turning his attention from the chicken, Ricky suddenly shouted, "Look up there! What's that?"

As the rest of the family looked, they passed something half-submerged in the water.

"An old rowboat," Mr. Hollister remarked. "Whoever owns it will probably never see it again."

142

"Say, that looks familiar," Pete remarked, looking intently. "I think it's——"

"The old rowboat that Bobby Reed set off in," Pam added excitedly.

"Are you sure? How can you tell?" Mrs. Hollister asked.

"By the old rusty ring in the prow," Pete told her. "I've never seen another boat with an iron ring like that one."

As the old boat drifted closer, the children were certain that it was the same one that they had seen half-buried in the mud near the Stone Bridge at Shoreham.

Though no one spoke, all the Hollisters were thinking the same thing. Maybe Bobby Reed had fallen overboard! Had something terrible happened to him? Oh, they hoped he had only abandoned the boat somewhere along the shore.

Pete looked at his father. "Don't you think we ought to search the shore nearby?" he asked. "This is near Fleetwood, isn't it, where Uncle Russ made the picture of Bobby."

"Yes." Mr. Hollister smiled. "This is your trip, Pete. If you think there's a chance of finding Bobby, we'll certainly take a look. Which shore shall we investigate first?"

"The west bank, Dad. Bobby's boat was closer to that side."

Mr. Hollister veered in that direction, and they searched up and down for half a mile, calling to

"Say, that looks familiar," Pete cried.

campers along the shore. No one had seen the boy.

As the *Sweetie Pie* turned toward the east bank,
Mrs. Hollister tuned in the radio. Everyone listened
attentively to the local newscast which began by saying Bobby had not been seen nor heard from.

"We've just got to find him!" Pam declared suddenly. "What'll we do?"

By this time, they had reached the east shore, and
the search went on. But again the Hollisters were disappointed. Mr. Hollister steered back to the channel,
and they started downstream.

"Let's play 'hide the dolly'," Sue suggested to
Holly, and the two girls went down to their bunk.

But, in a few minutes, they decided instead to go
to the galley and get some crackers for themselves and
their babies. Just as Holly stepped into the *Sweetie*

Pie's kitchen, the boat gave a great lurch. The sliding door slammed shut.

Sue fell down but picked herself up at once. She tried to open the door but could not do it.

"Holly, let me in," she called out.

"I—I can't. The door's stuck!"

At this moment, Ricky came to the galley. Sue asked him to try the door. The boy tugged at it with all his might. The door did not budge.

By this time, Holly was becoming frightened. "Go get Daddy!" she said.

Ricky raced up the steps and told his father. At once, Mr. Hollister throttled down his speed and told Pete to take the wheel. Then he jumped down into the cabin and tried the door.

He could not slide it back either!

"Oh, Daddy," Sue cried, "can't you get Holly out?"

CHAPTER 15

A Water Cowboy

"I'LL GET you out of that locked galley in a second, Holly," her father called. "Uncle Russ gave me a set of keys."

Mr. Hollister pulled out a key ring. He inserted each one into the lock and turned it. Nothing happened.

"The door must have bolted itself from the other side," he groaned.

Mr. Hollister told Holly how to slip the bolt, but she kept declaring there was nothing to slip.

"I guess we'll have to break down the door," her father said.

"Oh, that would be terrible," his wife spoke up. "I wouldn't want to damage Russ's nice boat. There must be some other way."

By this time Pete, Pam and Ricky had crowded around. Pete had set the wheel so it would not move. Each one tried to figure out how to release Holly. Suddenly Pete cried:

"I know a way! The ventilator!"

"You mean that hole in the top of the cabin with the fan in it?" Pam asked.

"Yes. Couldn't we take it out, Dad, and I could squeeze through?"

"Well, maybe," his father agreed.

They stepped upon the catwalk and examined the ventilator.

"I guess we could remove these screws," Mr. Hollister said. Then he added doubtfully, "But the tools are in the galley!"

"Not all of them," Pete said, grinning. "There's another box of them in the engine pit."

He got the box. While the others called encouragement to Holly, he and his father went to work. They had to take the fan apart before they were able to remove it.

"I hope we can get this together again," Pete chuckled, as he started to lower himself through the opening. "Holly, where am I?"

"Right over the stove," she answered. "Swing a little to the left. Now forward a tiny bit."

She reached up and grabbed his ankles so his feet would not touch the burners. In a moment, he had jumped down and was standing beside his sister.

"Oh Pete, get me out of here!" Holly begged him.

"Sure thing, Sis."

He tried to shove the door, but it refused to move. And the catch was stuck tight.

"I guess you'll have to climb out the hole up there," Pete told Holly and boosted her to the roof.

Mr. Hollister pulled his daughter through the opening, and she took a deep breath of fresh air.

"Holly, where am I?"

"I'm so glad to be out," she said. "It—it wasn't nice in there all alone."

Meanwhile Pete had taken out the tool kit in the galley and was trying to release the jammed lock. He used a screw driver, then a little wedge. Neither worked. Finally a thin piece of wire which he bent into a hook did the trick. Pete slid the door back and fastened it.

"Thank goodness," said his father. "Now we'll put the ventilator back."

"While I get my starving family something to eat," Mrs. Hollister laughed. "Do you realize it's two-thirty?"

After eating, everyone rested, then they went for swims. Finally as the family was ready to start off again, a radio report came on that revealed Bobby Reed was still missing.

"But I have a feeling we're going to find him soon," Pam stated. "By tomorrow sure."

"I think so too," Pete said. "Dad, that place where those boys saw the strange old man must be near here. Let's stay close to shore and go slow."

"Okay, son, and everyone look hard."

Mr. Hollister kept the *Sweetie Pie* throttled down so they could not miss an inch of either shore. The scenery along the river became wilder. There were no cabins, trees grew close together and bushes were thickly matted.

"This looks like the spot where Old Moe might be, Dad!" Pete said excitedly. When his father paid no attention, he turned to look at him. Mr. Hollister was

"Old Moe might be here, Dad!"

frowning deeply, and there was a worried expression on his face.

"Why Dad, what's the matter?" he asked.

"Our fuel tank's empty!" his father answered.

He had barely said this when the engine sputtered and died.

"This is a fine place to be stuck," Mr. Hollister said in disgust. "A great skipper I turned out to be."

"I know where there's a gas station," Ricky spoke up.

"So do I. Lots of 'em," Pete said. "But what good will they do us?"

"I mean a water one," Ricky went on. "I saw it back there." He pointed up the river. "We could row to it."

"You're a lifesaver, Ricky," his mother said, hugging him.

Mr. Hollister and Pete lowered the rowboat and went off to get some gasoline, telling the attendant who they were and explaining their predicament. Half an hour later they returned with a can of fuel. When it was in the tank, Mr. Hollister ran the cruiser up to the marine gasoline station.

"Hello folks," the attendant called. "Glad to serve the Happy Hollisters," he said.

"How did you know we're called that?" Pam asked, amazed.

"Don't you think I could guess it?" the man teased. "You all look pretty contented."

"I'll bet a river frog the lad is Bobby."

"We're really sad," Sue spoke up. "We can't find Bobby."

Holly explained why they were looking for him. The station attendant pushed back his cap.

"I'll bet a river frog the lad who told me about you nice folks is your Bobby."

"What!" Pete cried. "Bobby was here?"

"That's right. He said you Happy Hollisters had been real kind to him."

"Where'd he go?" Pete asked excitedly.

"Sorry, son, but I don't know. He just said he was out fishin' and lookin' for the biggest Clown Fish in this river."

"Was he in a rowboat?"

"No, he was walking."

"Then Bobby is all right!" Pam cried in delight.

"And he must be somewhere around here!"

It was decided to do a little hiking inland to look for the boy. Mr. Hollister led the four older children through the woods. But the brambles tore their clothes so badly that they had to turn back.

"I'm sure Bobby couldn't be here after all," Pam declared.

As soon as they reached the *Sweetie Pie*, Mr. Hollister started the engine and went off, waving to the man at the station.

"It's getting late," his wife said presently. "I think we'd better stop for the night soon."

"How about that place across the river where the old man might be?" Pete suggested.

"If there's a sheltered spot near it, we'll moor," his father agreed.

They crossed the river and hugged the shore for a distance. Suddenly Ricky, sitting up at the very end of the prow, cried out:

"Cove ahead!"

Mr. Hollister followed his son's gaze. To their left was a small inlet, almost hidden from view by tall trees along the river bank.

"This is a good spot," Mr. Hollister agreed, as they reached it.

The water swirled and eddied about, but it was not as swift as the current in the river.

"Okay, drop anchor!" Mr. Hollister ordered.

"Right, Skipper," Ricky replied, as he and Pam dropped the anchor over.

Ricky and Pam dropped the anchor over.

Pete wanted to explore the area at once, but it was growing dusk, and his parents felt he should wait until morning. Mrs. Hollister and Pam cooked supper, and after they had eaten it, the children played on deck for awhile. Ricky found a rope and pretended to be a cowboy lassoing cattle.

"Look out, cow!" he called to Sue. "I'll get you!"

"I'm not a cow," she said indignantly.

After awhile, Mrs. Hollister reminded them that it was bedtime. As she did, the wind began to blow again. In a few minutes, it was as strong as it had been the night before.

Suddenly one of the wicker chairs on the deck was blown off into the water.

Ricky was standing nearby when this happened, and he went into action before the chair might sink.

Quickly using his lasso, he caught the chair and lifted it back to the boat.

"You're a good cowboy," Sue told him. "A water cowboy."

The others laughed and then went to bed.

In the middle of the night the lightning and thunder increased in fury. Rain fell in torrents. Suddenly there was a blinding flash of lightning, followed instantly by a tremendous clap of thunder.

It awakened everyone immediately, just in time for them to hear a cracking sound. The lightning had hit a big tree on the shore, splitting it down the middle! It fell into the water with a great splash, rocking the boat violently.

Everyone sat bolt upright in their bunks. Mr. and Mrs. Hollister asked quickly if the children were all right. Each one nodded but reported having felt a tingling sensation.

"That was the lightning," Mrs. Hollister said. "We can probably thank that tree for saving our lives."

When the storm subsided, Pete and his father donned raincoats and went up to the deck with flashlights. One half of the big tree was lying alongside their boat.

"Whew! That was a close one!" Mr. Hollister exclaimed. "I hope that trunk won't make it difficult for us to get out of here," he added, as they came back.

"Now we must all go to sleep again," Mrs. Hollister said.

Pete found it hard to do so. He kept thinking how

"Whew! That was a close one!"

dreadful it would be if the *Sweetie Pie* were caught. What would Uncle Russ think?

He would fall asleep then soon wake up again. When he awakened for the sixth time, he noticed that the luminous clock on the wall said four o'clock. Suddenly he was startled by a thump against the side of the boat. He got up at once. On the steps he met his father.

"What is it, Dad?"

CHAPTER 16

An Exciting Search

PETE and his father wondered if a piece of floating wood had bumped into the side of the cruiser, as they beamed their flashlights over the side of the *Sweetie Pie.*

"See anything, Dad?" his son asked.

"No. Do you?"

"No. Maybe it was a sharp log."

"You don't suppose someone in a boat———"

The words were hardly out of Mr. Hollister's mouth when they heard the soft dipping of oars. Both turned their lights in the direction of the sound. They could see nothing, and, in a moment, everything was quiet.

"Dad, someone was prowling around our boat!" Pete exclaimed.

"I'm afraid so. And he evidently didn't want to be seen."

"But why?" Pete asked.

"Maybe he thought no one would be on board in such a bad storm," his father replied. "That would make it a good chance to break into the cabin and steal some of the equipment."

"It's a lucky thing we were here and heard him," Pete said.

Mr. Hollister decided to stay up the rest of the night and watch. He told his son to return to bed.

There was bright sunlight when Pete awakened again. As he got up, Ricky awoke. The boys dressed and hurried to the deck.

Their father was glad to see them and said he would go now and get some sleep. Nothing had happened while he was on watch, but in the distance through the woods he had seen a flickering light.

"I'll bet someone's camping there," said Ricky.

"Or it could have been in a cabin; maybe Old Moe's," Pete suggested excitedly. "May we go look, Dad?"

"All right. But be careful."

"This makes a swell bridge!"

At this moment, Mrs. Hollister appeared. She said any search must come after breakfast, so the children helped her prepare it. In their eagerness to be off, they started to eat very fast, and she had to warn them to slow down.

When the four older children were ready to leave, Ricky stepped onto the split tree trunk alongside the boat.

"Yikes!" he exclaimed. "This makes a swell bridge right to shore. Come on, kids!"

Balancing like a tightrope walker, Ricky crossed the trunk. Pete and the two girls followed. Once Ricky teetered and nearly fell into the river, but he recovered his balance just in time.

"Crickets!" he exclaimed, reaching the shore, "this sure is fun." Suddenly he let out a whoop. "See all the fish!"

"Where?"

He pointed down into the water. "Right here. They're in a wire pen."

The other children scrambled along the tree trunk to where Ricky was standing.

Below them, in a wire crib, was a sight they had never seen before. Hundreds of Clown Fish were swimming about. They were of all sizes, from six inches long to twenty-five inches.

"They're giants," Holly remarked.

"The fish aren't tagged," said Pete, "but do you suppose they belong to Old Moe?"

Splash!

"Oh, I hope so," Pam replied. "If we find him, we'll get the reward offered by Mr. Finder."

Meanwhile Ricky had picked a leaf off one of the branches and thrown it into the crib. The fish evidently thought it was food, and wiggled up to nibble it.

"Say," Ricky exclaimed, "all we have to do is net one of these for our tank at *The Trading Post*."

Holly stared at the fish, fascinated. They swirled about so fast that she said they made her dizzy.

"If you fell in there with those hungry fish," Pete said with a chuckle, "they sure would pull your pigtails."

Pam and Ricky laughed, but not Holly. She suddenly had leaned too far forward and now was trying desperately to keep from falling into the fish pen.

Splash!

The fish scurried in every direction as Holly went under. Pete bent down and helped her climb back.

"Ugh!" she said, spluttering. "That water tastes awful!"

"You mean you don't like raw fish?" Pete grinned.

Holly made a face at her brother, then asked them all to wait for her while she went to change her clothes.

"Okay. We'll walk slow," Pam promised.

Her sister hurried back, and the others jumped to the embankment. The trees and bushes were so thick it was hard to see far ahead. But there were two very narrow trails. One led along the shore, the other directly among the trees.

As the children waited for Holly, Pete heard a rustling sound. Turning, he could just barely make out a figure some distance up the shore trail. The next second it disappeared completely.

"I'm going after him!" Pete cried out. "Come on, Ricky. Pam, you wait for Holly."

As the boys ran, Ricky said, "I wonder if we can catch him. If he's Old Moe, maybe he can't run fast."

Running was not easy, because the path was covered with wet, slippery leaves. Once Ricky skidded and fell flat. Pete waited for him to get up and the younger boy said dolefully:

"Now that man's far ahead of us."

"Perhaps we can pick up his footprints," Pete suggested hopefully. "There's a muddy place up ahead."

When they reached it, Pete whistled in surprise.

He pointed out footprints in the mud. Several sets had been made by the same man, but one of the prints was from a boy's moccasins.

"Oh, boy!" Ricky exclaimed, "Bobby wore moccasins at our house. This is a real detective's clue!" Then he looked off into the wood and shouted, "Bobby! Bobby! Where are you?"

The only answer was a faint echo of his own voice. The boys started to follow the footprints. To their amazement those of the boy suddenly ended.

"Maybe he climbed a tree," Ricky suggested, looking up.

They saw no one hidden among the branches, however. After a moment Pete said:

"I know what. The man must have carried the boy."

Pete pointed out footprints in the mud.

Eagerly the Hollister brothers followed the man's footprints. Presently the path turned into the woods and became so overgrown with moss and grass that Pete decided they must have taken a wrong turn. The footprints were gone."

"What'll we do?" Ricky asked his brother.

"I guess we'll have to go back," Pete decided, and started for the boat.

Meanwhile, Holly had changed her clothes and now waited with Pam for the boys to return.

"I wonder if they found that man," Pam said, explaining about the person on the shore trail. "If he was only Old Moe——"

"Where do you suppose this other trail goes?" Holly asked. "To Old Moe's cabin, maybe?"

"Let's walk along a little way and try to find out," Pam said impatiently.

They started off, but found the trail full of sharp stones which made them turn their ankles and hurt their feet. They kept their eyes down to avoid the stones.

For this reason they did not notice someone watching them from up ahead. As Pam looked up suddenly, she gave a little scream.

Beside the path and peering at the girls from between two bushes stood a strange old man. He had white hair and a long flowing beard, deep set dark eyes and a thin nose.

The old man was shabbily dressed. In his right

"Run!" the old man ordered.

hand, he held a crooked cane. He lifted it menacingly toward the children who stopped short and stared at him.

"Hello," Holly ventured timidly, gulping with surprise.

The man said nothing, merely glaring at the Hollisters.

"You—you wouldn't hurt us, would you?" Holly continued bravely.

The old man took a step forward, the cane still held over his head.

"Come on!" Pam whispered to her sister. "We'd better go back."

Suddenly the stranger's eyes flashed.

"Go away! Go away!" he shouted in a high pitched voice. "You have no business here!"

CHAPTER 17

A Telltale Cane

THE OLD man began to wave the cane at Pam and Holly.

"Run!" he ordered.

The girls became frightened. Turning, they began running as fast as they could. Every so often they would look back to see whether he was coming after them.

"I don't see him now," Pam said presently. "Let's go back!"

Holly was not sure they should, but followed her sister and they retraced their steps. The old man still stood in the same spot.

"Didn't I tell you not to come here?" he cried. "You go get on your boat and leave at once!"

Pam stood her ground. "Why?" she asked him bravely.

"I won't tell you!" the old man replied stubbornly.

With this he waved his cane again and came toward the girls. This time when they turned and ran, he followed them. He could not run as fast as they, but he did not stop.

"Oh, maybe he'll make Daddy move the boat right

away!" Holly said fearfully. "Then we never can find Old Moe or Bobby Reed."

"Daddy can talk to him better than we can," replied Pam.

She turned around to see how close the old man was. At this very second she saw him trip, wave his arms a moment, and then fall flat. He did not get up.

"Oh, Holly, he's hurt himself!" Pam cried, as she stopped running.

Holly stopped too, and they hurried back toward the old man who was still lying on the ground. He had a big bump on his forehead.

"Oh, he hit his head on a stone," Pam said. "He's unconscious. We must do something for him."

"What?" Holly asked.

Pam looked around. Nearby was a sparkling stream of water. She took a clean handkerchief from her pocket and asked Holly to soak it in the water. Holly did this and when she returned with it, Pam laid it on the man's forehead.

Then she tried some little first-aid tricks she had learned—patting his cheeks and rubbing his wrists, but he did not regain consciousness. Pam became frightened.

"We must get Mother here at once," she declared.

Just as the girls were about to leave, Holly noticed the man's cane. Initials had been burnt into the stick.

"Pam, look!" she said. "The initials on this are M.T. Do you suppose that could be for Moses Twigg?"

"It probably is," Pam agreed excitedly. "Come on, we must hurry."

The two girls ran all the way back to the tree bridge, climbed up on it and started for the *Sweetie Pie*. Pam began calling loudly.

"Mother! Mother! Come here quick!"

Mrs. Hollister hurried from the cabin as well as the children's father.

"What's the matter?" they asked together.

Quickly Pam explained about the old man. Mrs. Hollister dashed inside the cruiser to get the first-aid kit. Then they all started off, including Sue.

As they reached the path, Pete and Ricky returned. Upon hearing the story, they decided to go along too.

"He's just up ahead!" cried Pam, who was leading the procession.

He held his head and moaned.

She turned a curve in the trail and stared in blank astonishment. The old man was gone!

"He went away!" she cried. "But where could he go?"

The Hollisters stood still for several seconds, then decided the old man must have gone to his cabin. They hurried along the trail and several minutes later saw a little log dwelling. Mr. Hollister knocked on the door.

There was no answer and after repeated knocking, he opened the door and walked in. Seated in a rocking chair was the white-bearded old man. He held his head in his hands and was moaning. Seeing his visitors, he said wearily:

"Go away! I don't want anybody here!"

Mrs. Hollister paid no attention. She walked up to him and laid her hand on his shoulder. "We've come to help you," she said gently. "My daughters tell me you fell and hurt yourself."

"Yes, I bumped my head," he admitted. "It aches badly."

Mrs. Hollister opened the first-aid kit and started to work. In a short time, she had put lotion on the bruise and bandaged the man's head. Then she got a glass of water and gave him a little tablet. In a few moments he said he felt better and thanked her. He even smiled warmly.

"I didn't mean to be ungrateful," the old man said. "I've lived alone so long, I guess I'm not very polite any more."

167

"Please don't cry, Mr. Snow Beard."

Rather abruptly Pete stepped forward and said to
him, "Aren't you Moses Twigg?"

The old man gave a start of surprise. "That's my
name, but how did you know it? I have kept it a secret
for many, many years."

Pete told about the Clown Fish he had caught up
in Shoreham, and how many people were puzzled
about the strange tags on the fishes' tails. When the
old man heard this he smiled.

"These fish are my pets," he said. "By cross breed-
ing, I have developed what you call the Clown Fish,
which I hope many sportsmen will enjoy catching. A
few of them which I had tagged got away from me."

"Did you bump into our boat about four o'clock
this morning?" Pete asked him.

"Yes, I have an ancient rowboat hidden among the trees. I was trying to find out about you folks."

The children explained how they had put their clues together to guess that the old man was Moses Twigg.

"But the funniest thing of all," Ricky piped up, "is about your money in the bank."

Old Moe looked up in amazement. "Money in the bank?"

"Yes," Pete continued. "You left your money there a long time ago. Mr. Finder is looking for you. He wants to give it to you before twenty years are up."

The old man was so taken aback by this announcement that he buried his bushy face in his hands, saying his memory had not been good since he had grown older.

"Please don't cry, Mr. Snow Beard," Sue said, as she went up to him and put her hand on his shoulder.

The old man looked up, brushed away a tear, and smiled at the little girl.

"If you want," he said, "you may call me Old Moe. Everybody used to call me that." Sighing, he added, "I suppose I ought to have someone to take care of me."

"Maybe you will," Holly said. "Do you know that you have a great-grandson who is looking for you?"

"I certainly don't. Why, that's splendid! Where is he?"

"We don't know. He was in Shoreham but he ran away."

The old man hung his head in disappointment as Pam took up the story. She told how the boy's mother had come from the West to look for Moses Twigg, but had discovered that he had disappeared many years before. Now she was heartbroken because her son was gone too.

"Tell me," said Old Moe, "what is the name of my grandson, and how old is he?"

The children were amazed at his question. But they suddenly realized that he had not even known of his granddaughter's marriage.

"He's ten years old and his name's Bobby Reed," Pete spoke up.

"Bobby Reed!" Old Moe shouted, suddenly getting his strength back. "Bobby Reed!" He jumped from the chair. "Come here!" he ordered and led the way to a door leading to another room.

CHAPTER 18

The Prize

THE old man opened the door to his bedroom. Stretched out on a cot and sound asleep was Bobby Reed!

Before anyone could speak, the old man put his fingers to his lips and closed the door. Then he said:

"Is he my great-grandson?"

"Yes," the Hollisters said together.

Moses Twigg sat down in his rocking chair again. He asked them to tell him all they knew. He himself had little to reveal. While walking on the shore the afternoon before, he had come upon Bobby. The boy was crying and admitted that he was very hungry. He had said his name was Bobby Reed, which had meant nothing to Old Moe at that time.

"Of course, I didn't tell the lad my name," he said. "I've kept it a secret all these years. After my store burned, I seemed to lose interest in everything and decided to go away and live all alone.

"Well, about Bobby. The boy was so exhausted that I carried him most of the way to my cabin."

"That's why his footprints ended so suddenly," Pete remarked.

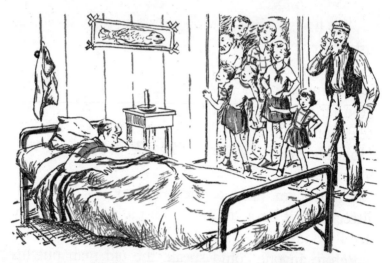

Bobby Reed was sound asleep.

Old Moe smiled. "I gave Bobby a good meal and put him to bed. He hasn't awakened yet."

Mrs. Hollister spoke up. "It's a miracle that you should have been the one to find him. You have no idea how many people have been looking for Bobby. I'm so glad that he's safe."

"We're all glad," Holly said.

"I have a suggestion," Mr. Hollister said. "Suppose we go back to the boat and after Bobby wakes up, Mr. Twigg, you bring him to the *Sweetie Pie*. In the meantime, I'll find a telephone and notify his mother that Bobby is safe."

Moses Twigg agreed to this plan, saying, "I know Bobby will be overjoyed to see his Hollister friends again."

"I'll have dinner waiting for all of us," Mrs. Hollister said.

As soon as they reached the *Sweetie Pie*, her husband suggested that he and Pete take the rowboat and go up the river until they came to a house that had a telephone. They lowered the boat and set off. Mr. Hollister rowed until he became weary, then Pete took a turn. Still they did not come to any cabins.

"This is really wild country down here," Mr. Hollister observed after awhile.

"I wonder if Old Moe will ever want to leave it," Pete said. "Probably Bobby's mother will want him to live with them, but I bet he'll be sorry to go away from the woods."

"I think you're right, son," Mr. Hollister agreed.

"Bobby! It sure is swell to see you again."

"A city would seem pretty stuffy to Old Moe now."

They rowed along in silence for another fifteen minutes, then at last Mr. Hollister saw a cabin. A wire running from it indicated it must have a telephone. Pete pulled into the dock, and they climbed out.

A pleasant-looking woman came to the door when they knocked and said she had a telephone which they might use.

"Suppose you put in the call, Pete," his father smiled. "After all, you and Ricky and the girls really solved this mystery."

He got in touch with the Shoreham Police and asked for Officer Cal. When he told his news, the policeman whistled.

"That's wonderful, Pete," he praised him. "I said you'd solve the mystery." Officer Cal promised to get in touch with Bobby's mother at once. He knew she would want to be at the Shoreham Municipal Pier when the *Sweetie Pie* docked. Did Pete have any idea when they would get back?

Pete turned to his father, "When do you think we'll reach Shoreham?" he asked.

"Well, I hope our boat's not trapped by that tree," Mr. Hollister replied. "But I'd say we can make Shoreham by evening."

His son told this to Officer Cal, and the policeman said he would go over to the Reed home at once.

"That's an amazing story," the woman said, as she accepted Mr. Hollister's money in payment for the telephone call. Then she waved good-by to them.

It did not take Pete and his father so long to get back to the *Sweetie Pie* as it had to find the telephone, because they went downstream. When they reached the boat, a surprise awaited them. Old Moe and Bobby Reed had come to the cruiser and now everyone was enjoying the big meal which Mrs. Hollister had prepared.

"Bobby!" Pete cried, going up to him. "It sure is swell to see you again!"

Bobby smiled. "This is the happiest day of my life, Pete," he said. He went on excitedly, not even pausing for breath, "I hear my mother's home, and I've found my great-grandfather, and he's going to let me catch the biggest fish in the Muskong River so I can win the prize at *The Trading Post.*"

Pete laughed. "We all hope you do," he said, as he helped himself to some potato salad.

During the meal several stories were exchanged. Bobby was amazed to hear how the Hollisters had been searching for him for days.

"I didn't mean to worry anybody," he explained. "I just wanted to try to find the biggest fish so that I could win the prize."

"Is that the only reason you ran away?" Ricky asked him.

"N-no, not the only one," replied Bobby. Then he told them that he did not want to live with Mr. Gillis any longer.

"Did you take the old boat from under the bridge?" Pam asked.

"Yes, I did. I made up my mind when I found a couple of old oars in the bushes. But I could hardly keep the old tub afloat 'cause she was leaking in all her seams."

"Did you lose the boat in the storm?" Ricky wanted to know.

Bobby said that he had. He had hit a rock and rammed a hole in the bottom.

"I had to let the old thing sink and swim ashore," he continued. "For two days I kept on walking through the woods, following the river. Once in awhile I met somebody who gave me food. But for one whole day I didn't have anything."

He looked at Old Moe and smiled. "That is," the boy added happily, "not until my great-grandfather found me."

As Old Moe beamed at him, Bobby declared proudly, "Old Moe is the best fisherman in the world. He has lots of different lures which'll catch any kind of fish in the Muskong River."

"Then he'll give you a great big fish so you'll win the prize at *The Trading Post*, won't he?" Ricky remarked.

Old Moe held up his hand. "No," he said, firmly. "If Bobby wants to win that prize, he'll have to catch the fish all by himself."

"That's right," Mr. Hollister agreed.

Old Moe told them that he knew of a pool down the river about half a mile where there was a whopper of a Clown Fish.

"I tried to catch him myself, but he broke one of my lines. I was going to try to catch him today. But it'll be fine if Bobby does it."

As the meal ended, plans were made for all of them to go back to Shoreham on the *Sweetie Pie*.

"I know your mother will be so happy to see you, Bobby," Mrs. Hollister said, beaming.

"And we've solved another mystery," Ricky said gleefully. "Won't Officer Cal be glad to hear about this?"

"We've found all we set out for," Pam said dreamily.

Ricky spoke up quickly. "Oh no, we haven't," he said, grinning. "I haven't found a lopadupalus for Mr. Kent."

"It has two heads," Ricky said.

When Old Moe heard this, he scratched his head. "A lopadupalus?" he asked. "What's that?"

Pete winked at the old man, and told him that it was some kind of creature that the nice editor wanted for his aquarium.

"Now, say," Old Moe said with a big grin, "I think I know what you want. Come, follow me, Ricky."

All the children followed him. Old Moe led them to a spring a short distance in the woods.

"Now, if you look down in there," he said, "you will see a lopadupalus."

"I only see a turtle," Sue piped up.

"Me, too," Ricky said. "But it's the funniest one I've ever seen. It has two heads."

As he spoke the turtle swam to the surface of the spring. Indeed, it did have two heads, and the Hollisters laughed when they saw it.

"I didn't know a lopadupalus was a two-headed turtle," Ricky said, almost ready to believe the story.

Old Moe put his hand into the water. The turtle swam right into it.

"It has one head on the front and another on the back where the tail should be!" Ricky cried.

Holly looked so close that her nose nearly touched the turtle. "Is this what you call a freak of nature?" she asked.

"It is that," Old Moe said. "But I'm afraid I'll have to confess that I made the turtle that way. That head on the back of the turtle is made of wood, and I have a secret way of fastening it onto the turtle's shell."

178

What a tremendous bass it was!

He turned the turtle upside down. It did have a little tail, which was right under the make-believe head.

"This would be wonderful to give Mr. Kent," Ricky said, his eyes dancing.

"You may have him," Old Moe said, handing the turtle over.

"Oh boy, this is great!" Ricky cried. "Thanks a lot."

They returned to the *Sweetie Pie*, and Mr. Hollister said they must get started. Bobby still had to catch the big fish, and they might have trouble moving the cruiser.

While Bobby and Pete went back to Old Moe's cabin for a stout fish pole and a crate in which to keep the fish alive, Mr. Hollister and Old Moe cut away as many branches as they could from the fallen tree alongside the boat.

When Pete and Bobby returned, everyone got aboard and Mr. Hollister started the engine. A few tries and they were clear of the old tree. It was not long before they were out in the middle of the stream.

"Where does the big fish live?" Mr. Hollister asked Old Moe.

The old man pointed to a spot on the left bank. When they reached it, Mr. Hollister stopped and dropped anchor.

Old Moe handed Bobby Reed the fishing pole.

"Cast way over there, by that old stump," he directed.

Bobby made several casts, but did not come close enough to the stump. On the fourth try, though, the lure dropped right next to the stump. Immediately there was a great swish and a splash.

"He's got it! He's got it!" Ricky exclaimed.

Bobby battled the big fish as it swam back and forth and jumped from the water to try to shake the hook from its mouth. All the while Bobby kept reeling in.

Finally the big Clown Fish flopped over exhausted near the side of the boat, and Old Moe gave Bobby a net which he lowered to scoop up the fish.

What a tremendous bass it was!

"Golly! It'll touch both sides of our tank at The Trading Post," Ricky cried, as it was put into the crate and the lid fastened. Then the crate was put into the water and secured by long ropes to the railing of the boat.

"This will surely win the prize," Mr. Hollister said with a chuckle. "Any fish bigger than this, I would call a whale."

Up the river they all went, singing songs on the way. It was late in the afternoon when they arrived at Shoreham's municipal dock.

"There's my mother!" Bobby cried, hurrying off the cruiser, with the others following.

When Mrs. Reed saw her son, she flung her arms around him, weeping and laughing all at the same time.

"Oh, I'm so glad you're safe! And these are your friends, the Hollisters. What splendid friends they are!"

Mrs. Reed turned to Bobby's great-grandfather and hugged him, saying she could hardly believe her good fortune.

"This is so wonderful!" she kept repeating.

"And we're going to live with him," said Bobby, "in a nice new house down the river. Great-grand-father told me."

The next day the newspaper carried a big story about the rescue of Bobby Reed and the finding of old Moses Twigg. It told how the Hollister children had won the reward Mr. Finder had offered and how they in turn had said it was to go to Bobby.

The bass contest was more successful than Mr. Hollister had ever thought possible. He had had to

"Oh, I'm so glad you're safe!"

rent a very large tank from a fish store to hold all the fish that were brought in. When the final day came, the children rushed down to *The Trading Post* to see who had won. In the window was a sign which read:

PRIZE FOR THE LARGEST

CLOWN FISH

CAUGHT IN THE MUSKONG RIVER

WON BY

BOBBY REED

"Hurrah!" cried Ricky and the others joined in.
"Thanks," said a voice behind them.
They turned to see the smiling face of their new

friend Bobby, and told him how glad they were he had won.

"Come in and see what my prize is," he said.

"I'll bet it'll be a fish pole," Ricky guessed.

"No," Bobby answered. "Your father says I may have a rowboat to go with our new home. We're moving tomorrow. Be sure to come and see us."

"We will."

Two days later Uncle Russ returned to pick up his boat. He was so happy that everyone was safe and the children had found Bobby Reed, he said he did not mind a few scratches on the *Sweetie Pie*. After he left, Ricky announced rather abruptly:

"I just found out Mr. Kent's home from his vacation. I have to go see him."

The other children giggled, because they knew why. All five of them went to the newspaper office, and were ushered in to Mr. Kent's office.

"Well, what can I do for you today?" he asked with a big smile.

Ricky stepped forward. "I have something for you, Mr. Kent," he said, holding one hand behind his back.

"What is it, son?"

Ricky held the two-headed turtle toward him.

"Here's your lopadupalus," he said.

Mr. Kent's jaw dropped and his eyes popped. Then he joined the children in laughing when he heard about the discovery of the lopadupalus. Lifting the top off his aquarium, he put the turtle inside.

183

"Thanks to you, Ricky," he said, "I have the most unusual collection of reptiles in the world, I'm sure."

"Is there any other strange creature you want us to look for?" Ricky asked. "If there is, the Happy Hollisters will find it for you."